Haunted
by the Past

A Novella

by

Kelly Hagen

Haunted by the Past
A Novella
By Kelly Hagen

©2013 Kelly Hagen

This book is a work of fiction. Names, characters, places, and incidents are a product of the author's imagination or are used fictitiously. Any resemblance to actual events, locales, or persons, living or dead, is coincidental.

Published by TreasureLine Publishing
www.TreasureLinePublishing.weebly.com

Edited by Mary Campagna Findley

ISBN: 978-1-61752-164-5

Also available in eBook publication

PRINTED IN THE UNITED STATES OF AMERICA

This book is dedicated to my family and anyone else out there that has ever faced the unknown and overcome it by holding on to Jesus.

"Trust in the Lord with all thine heart;
and lean not unto thine own understanding.
In all thy ways acknowledge him,
and he shall direct thy paths."
Proverbs 3:5-6 (KJV)

"Haunted by the Past" is a great read! I couldn't put it down! I love how fast the author leads us into the suspense. It's well written and keeps you anticipating what's going to happen next. I also enjoyed the romance between Nadia and Trent, and how God led them to each other at just the right time. I highly recommend this powerful and entertaining read!

Amanda Beth - Christian author

Chapter 1

Ring...ring...ring...

Stomach in knots, Nadia slowly reached for the phone.

"Hello?"

Silence.

"Hello, who is this? What do you want?"

Silence.

"Not again!"

Her knotted stomach sent a salty taste to her mouth.

Slamming down the phone, she ran to the bathroom. Her clammy hands gripped the hard gray marble sink. She raised her head but didn't recognize the face staring back at her. Just a hollow shell remained of the fun-loving girl she had been.

She tucked a strand of long brown hair behind her ear and wiped her moist, deep brown, empty-looking eyes. She breathed one slow, controlled breath at time until her rattled nerves settled down.

This was getting the best of her.

She forced her feet to carry her back to bed. The soft, purple, satin sheet brushed against her skin as she pulled it up over her. She stared at the ceiling. Thoughts of her simple childhood flooded her memory. *Why couldn't things be like that again?* Finally her mind could no longer fight off the sleep her body craved. Her eyelids fought against the downward pull. They lost.

Her eyes squinted at the beam of light that shone through the slender opening of the pale pink curtains. Morning had come too soon. The warmth on her face felt nice but she grumbled as she rolled over, eyes barely opened, and looked at the old, battered clock sitting on her nightstand. *What's another day on only a couple hours of sleep? It's overrated anyway.* She tossed the sheet aside and stretched, bringing each muscle out of its slumber, and then rubbed her eyes. She opened the dresser drawer, grabbed her Bible, and flipped it opened to her favorite book; Psalms, thankful for the peace it brought. She laid the Bible on her bed and prayed. The day awaited her.

Constant beeps met her ears as she stepped out of the shower. *Who called anybody this early in the morning?* She made her way to the nightstand and pressed the play button.

"Hi, Nadia, It's Mindy. I'm sorry for not calling sooner. I've been real busy showing houses. Anyway, hope you're settled in and love your new home. I have some days off next week if you still want me to show you around town. Oh, and I'm so glad you moved here. I missed you. Of course, I miss Pine Ridge, too; that's home. Give me call. I look forward to hearing from you."

Nadia thought back to the warm memories of her childhood in Pine Ridge. Every night she climbed up on her daddy's lap and listened attentively as he told about his day, while the smell of dinner filled the air. Her eyes shut tight over the tears that threatened to break through the composed face she fought to maintain. She rubbed away the goosebumps on her upper arms. *I miss Pine Ridge too, Mindy.*

Nadia breathed deep, forced her usual smile, and held her head high as she walked into "Caldwell and Associates". If she had learned anything over the last six weeks, it was that Mr. Caldwell expected her best. *I admire him though, the owner of a multi-million dollar company...Impressive.*

A slight grin crossed her face. Mr. Caldwell's tall, thin stature and thick, snow-white hair reminded her of her father, Samuel Lucas. He had been a kindhearted man with unshakable faith. She prayed to be the same. Quickly she wiped away the tear that escaped as she heard the door behind her open. Had it really been three years since her parents' accident?

She veered left. The clicking of her two-inch heels on the stone tile floor echoed through the hallway. *Why do I always have to be so emotional?* She pushed open the door and flipped on the lights. *Time to turn off the waterworks and get to work.* The door closed on its own behind her.

Her finger slid across the desk calendar to today's date, Thursday, October 25.. *Meeting with Mr. Caldwell, ten-thirty.* Her finger stopped again on Friday. *Lunch with Trent.*

Memory took her back to their first meeting. It was after the meet-and-greet with Mr. Caldwell and the "higher-ups" in the company. Her hands were full of pamphlets, notes, and folders that covered the details of her job and what was expected of her. The folders under her arm had started to slip on her way out of the conference room. Looking down, she had grabbed for them, not noticing the wall of a man blocking the hallway. She raised her head, eyes traveling upward, meaning to apologize, but the words would not form on her tongue. He was so *tall,* and had eyes a deeper brown than her own. His wavy hair fell perfectly on his white collar, and he had a smile that had to drive every woman to act like a giddy schoolgirl.

"Excuse me, miss; I should have been paying more attention to where I was going." Her hand met his. "My name is Trent Macalister."

"It really wasn't your fault. These folders were slipping." She shook her head. "Anyway, I'm Nadia Lucas."

"First day on the job, huh?"

"Is it that obvious?"

"Don't worry, things get better."

"Thanks, I hope so."

"Hey, would you like to sit with us at lunch?" Her eyes focused on the group of people behind him that she hadn't seen around his broad shoulders.

"Oh, wow, that's nice. I would love to."

"Great. I'll stop by your office around noon then."

"Okay."

Her heart had never skipped a beat until that moment.

She hated to admit it, but she was looking forward to lunch with Trent, away from the chaos of the corporate cafeteria. Not that she didn't enjoy the others' company; they had all made her feel welcome. There was just something about Trent that made her feel alive again…even if it was only for the time they were together.

"Excuse me, Ms. Lucas."

Hot liquid splashed Nadia's hand and sprayed over her desk. "Shoot!" Nadia set the coffee cup down and grabbed some paper towels.

"Oh, Ms. Lucas, I'm so sorry. I didn't mean to scare you. Here, let me wipe that up for you."

On the other side of her desk stood a five- foot-five redhead with an apologetic look on her face.

"It was my own fault, Jenny. I had my mind on something besides work. What did you need?"

"Oh, I just wanted to remind you of your appointment with Mr. Caldwell, but I see it's written in on your calendar."

Nadia's gaze fell to her watch. "Is it really ten already?"

"Yes, ma'am, it is."

"Thank you, Jenny, you've helped me so much these past two weeks."

"Well, thank you, Ms. Lucas."

Nadia rolled her shoulders up and swiveled her neck, trying to relieve some built-up tension. "I haven't been working here long, but I already feel like it's been years." She sighed.

"Hey, Nadia." Trent smiled as he walked through the door. "This package was sitting on a bench in the lobby. It's addressed to *Nadia Comings*, but you're the only Nadia I know who works here, so I thought I'd see if it was yours."

Hesitantly Nadia took the box from his outstretched hands. *Why would something with that name come here?* "Yes, that's me."

"Are you all right? You look like you've seen a ghost."

"I'm fine, Trent, thanks." A forced smile made its way to her face, but that *ghost* comment was closer to the truth than Trent knew.

She squirmed under his open but skeptical gaze. *How can I make him believe something I don't believe myself?* "Trent, this is Jenny Ryder, my new assistant. She's been with me for two weeks now. I know you've heard me talk about her, but can't remember if you've met yet or not."

"Yes, we've met. She ate lunch with us a couple times last week."

Shoot, how could I have forgotten about that? "Sorry, it's been a long week."

"Anyway, it's nice to see you again, Jenny." He nodded and smiled. "I better get back to work now."

Relief washed over Nadia's face until he turned back around.

"Oh, wait a minute, I almost forgot. We're still on for lunch Friday, right?"

"Yep, sure are."

"Great. See you later."

She made sure he walked all the way out the door this time, then focused her attention on the package that sat on her desk. Slowly sitting down, staring into outer space, her mind slipped back in time.

Her stomach did flip flops every time she heard his keys jingling in the door.

Hi, honey." Eric tossed the mail on the table and

kicked off his shoes.

"Hi, Eric. I missed you so much today." Nadia smiled and threw her arms around his neck.

Eric kissed her cheek. "What's for dinner?"

"Your favorite, of course; meatloaf, green beans, and mashed potatoes."

"You are the best wife ever!" He pulled her close and tucked her hair behind her ear.

"Mr. Comings, you are one crazy man!"

"Crazy over you, Mrs. Comings."

"You better be, if you know what's good for you."

"Oh, I know what's good for me, Nadia. It's you. I'm crazy over you, and only you. I'm the luckiest man alive."

She stared into his piercing blue eyes. She had never felt so safe: so happy.

"Ms. Lucas, are you ready? The meeting starts in five minutes." Her mind jolted back to the present as she shook off the memory. She looked again at the package. Her heart raced. Slowly her fingers ran over the name that had so recently belonged to her.

She picked the box up and shoved it away in a file drawer, locking it out of her sight, and she hoped, out of her mind's eye too.

"Well, let's get going. We do not want to keep Mr. Caldwell waiting."

Nadia walked through as Jenny held the door open. "Right behind you, boss."

Nadia held her head high and walked with confidence, even though the box event and the memory had left her with a tremendous ache in her stomach.

Pulling out the nearest chair on her side of the

long table, Nadia sat down, making small talk with Jenny while they waited. The atmosphere in the room shifted and ended their conversation when Mr. Caldwell cleared his throat. He laid a folder on the table in front him and nodded in their direction.

"Nadia, your work as Development Officer has been excellent the last couple weeks. Keep it up. I plan on getting another website up and running for our latest product. You'll find all the information you need in here." Nadia stopped the folder's sudden slide across the table with her hand. "If you should have any questions, well, ask. I want to see something on my desk by next Friday. That's all."

"Well, at least that didn't last long – I guess." Looking over at Jenny, she shrugged her shoulders and picked up the folder. *What a lovely way to start the day.*

"Wonder what his problem is this morning? I don't know that I've ever seen him that abrupt."

"I don't know, Jenny. Maybe he's had a rough week already too. I know I can't wait until Friday. I need a relaxing weekend."

"Don't we all?"

"I suppose you're right. Well, I need to look over these papers and come up with something. Wish me luck."

"Good luck."

Frustrated, Nadia laid her pen down, and leaned back in her leather chair. She was getting nowhere on product details. Her thoughts were on the box locked up a few steps away. *Out of sight, out of mind is not working, Lord.*

She pushed herself back, glanced at the file cabinet and stood up. Her heart raced. *Do I really want to know what's in there?*

She inserted the key, unlocked the drawer and walked back to her chair. She took the scissors from the caddy on her desk and slit the tape, then pulled apart the flaps.

It was empty.

Cold tingling shot along her spine. A faint thud rang out as the box came to a sudden stop against the wall. "What's going on?" She closed her eyes, whispered a prayer and focused her attention again to the green folder in front of her. *Work is not going to wait for me to figure this out.*

The rest of the day dragged. Her thoughts went back and forth between work and the crushed box still lying on the floor.

I can't run again. Somehow I have to face whatever... whoever... this is.

Chapter 2

Nadia left a voicemail for Mindy asking if they could meet up Saturday, then made her way to work. Amazed at the clarity of mind a restful night's sleep could bring, she determined to work like crazy while the energy lasted. *Why didn't I think of unplugging the phone earlier?*

The morning passed quickly as the ideas swept from her mind to her pad of paper. It wasn't until her stomach growled that she realized what time it was getting to be.

"Ms. Lucas, I was wondering if you were going to come up for air and eat lunch today?"

Laughter escaped from Nadia's pressed-together lips. "Of course, Jenny. I was just writing down this last idea I had. I have to write things down before I forget them, you know."

"I wonder what's on the menu today. Hopefully something good. I'm starving."

"Um, I don't know. You'll have to tell me later."

Jenny shot her a puzzled look. "I thought you said you were eating lunch?"

"Oh, I am. Trent and I are going to the little café on the corner today."

"Oh, really? I see that now." Nadia followed Jenny's pointed finger. "Is this serious, with you and Mr. Macalister?"

Warmth filled Nadia's cheeks. "It's just lunch, Jenny."

"Uh-huh. If it was just lunch, why are your cheeks as red as my fingernails right now?"

Nadia laughed it off and changed the subject. *There was nothing there but friendship, right?* Why, then, was she excited, a little nervous even, at the thought of lunch with Trent today? What was it about him that made her feel alive again?

"You didn't hear a word I just said, did you?"

"What?" Nadia grabbed the pen on her desk and set it on top of the folder. "No, I'm sorry, I guess I didn't." She stood up and stacked the files and other things she would need to take home over the weekend, trying to act nonchalant. It wasn't working.

"I said, you are free after lunch today, so why not take the rest of the day off? I'll call Mr. Caldwell and get the ok while you're at lunch. I know you've had a rough week, and you've been working hard, so I don't see there being a problem with it as long as I let him know you're taking work home with you. I can call and let you know what he says."

"That sounds wonderful! Great thinking, Jenny."

"Yeah, you can light you some candles, take a nice, long, warm, bubble bath, order a pizza and…" she wiggled her eyebrows "…watch a romantic movie."

"That sounds perfect." Her eyebrow rose. "You can put to rest the 'romantic' stuff though, I told you, Mr. Macalister and I are just having lunch. And some nice quiet time home *alone,* with no distractions, would be nice."

"Looks like your lunch date has arrived."

Nadia finger-combed her hair free of her ears as Trent walked through the door.

"Oh, hi, Jenny."

"Hi Mr. Macalister, I was just on my way out. You all have a *nice time*."

"It's *just lunch*, Jenny!" Nadia spoke sharper than she had meant to, and she could have sworn Trent looked disappointed. Nevertheless, he managed to smile.

"Are you ready, Nadia?"

"Yep, just need to grab my purse."

She was halfway to the door before she realized Trent wasn't beside her. She turned. *Great, he sees the box. Why didn't I pick that up?*

"Trent, are you coming?"

He turned, facing her. "What happened with the box?"

"Oh, nothing. Come on, our lunch break isn't that long."

His head tilted. Concern filled his voice. "Over lunch, I hope you'll tell me what's going on."

"Can we please just go now?" Nadia demanded.

Trent held the restaurant door open for Nadia, and then she followed him back toward an empty corner booth. "How's this one?" Trent made way for a waitress laying out menus, silverware and napkins.

"It's perfect." Nadia slid across the bench seat. "I don't like being out in the middle of everything."

"I remembered that. Here's the menu."

Her hand brushed against his as she took it. Her eyes fixed briefly on his smile before she quickly looked away.

Trent took a bite of his salad and washed it down

with a gulp of soda. "Ok, you've sat silent long enough. Spill it."

Nadia's muscles tightened. Digging up some courage from another look into his inviting smile, she finally spoke. "Sunday night I watched the news before going to bed. I decided to stay up a little longer and watch the talk show that came on next. I guess I fell asleep, because my home phone ringing woke me up. It was one in the morning. You know that terrible feeling you get in your stomach when you *know* something bad has happened? Well, I had it. I picked up the phone as fast I could and said *hello*. There was no answer. I said *hello* again. Still no answer, so I hung up. I thought that maybe it was a wrong number, or some kids playing a prank. However, it has happened every night, same time, since then. I unplugged the phone last night so I could sleep."

Lifting her gaze, she met Trent's face. Her shaking hands fiddled with the tablecloth as she waited for his reply.

Trent's brow wrinkled. "One or two nights might be explained easily enough, but five nights, at the same time, is a little harder. I'm guessing you don't have Caller ID?"

"No, I don't get many calls on my home phone. Mostly just on my cell and my work phone."

"I think you should call the phone company when you get home and get Caller ID on your phone. That could solve the problem fairly easy."

"I don't know why I never thought of that. Good idea. I'm hoping to take the rest of the day off, so I'll call as soon as I get home."

The French fry, mid-way to Nadia's mouth never

reached its destination. It landed back on the plate in front of her. Her frozen posture and wide-eyed stare drew Trent's attention. "Nadia? What are you looking at?" She didn't answer. She finally blinked after a big hand waved in front of her face several times. "Are you all right?"

"Yeah, sorry. I just ... thought I saw someone I knew, that's all. So, these fries are really good, huh?"

"Yes they are." He looked her over before he continued. "Now, care to explain the box, and what you think is going on?"

Her phone saved her. She hurriedly chewed the fry she had just stuffed in her mouth. "Hello."

"Hi, Ms. Lucas, just wanted to let you know Mr. Caldwell said you could have the rest of the day off."

"That's great. Thanks for calling, Jenny. We are almost finished with lunch so I'll just head home afterwards."

"Sounds good. I'll see you on Monday."

"Oh, wait. I forgot the folders in my office, so I guess I'll be back anyway. I might as well just stay and work."

"Oh, no. You need this time to yourself. Tell you what. Give me your address and I'll drop them off tonight on my way home."

"Are you sure? I don't want to be any trouble for you."

"I'm positive. It's no trouble at all."

Nadia gave Jenny her address, thanked her, and hung up.

"I have some things to take care of after work; nothing that will take very long, and then I will come by and check on you, now that I know where you live."

Trent winked. "It's actually not very far from my apartment."

"You don't have to do that, Trent. I will be fine."

"I don't remember *asking*."

A sigh escaped her. "I guess there's no point in arguing, is there?"

"Nope. No point at all. I'll call you when I'm on my way. Now that we've settled that, what's the deal with the package?"

Nadia squirmed in her seat. "I don't know. It…it was empty."

"Empty?"

"Yep. You know; nothing in there. Empty."

"That's odd."

"Yeah, I know."

"I guess that's all the more reason for me to stop by, then."

Nadia couldn't take her eyes off him. He laid his fork on the empty plate and wiped his mouth.

"You better be getting back to work before you're late." She tapped her watch, trying to tease away the serious look on his face. "You have about ten minutes."

"I guess you're right. Don't forget to call the phone company when you get home."

"I won't. Promise."

"I'll see you later. I have a fun meeting at two or I'd be taking off for the rest of the day as well. Call me if you need me."

"I will. Have fun."

She laughed as he grimaced. "I'll try."

A smile crept to her lips as she watched him walk up to the cash register. *He is such a gentlemen.*

Chapter 3

Nadia leaned back against the door as she ran her hand through her hair. Letting her arms drop, she inhaled and let her keys clatter onto the little wooden table on the other side of the coat closet. Dark smudges sat under the eyes of that pale face looking back from the hall mirror. Make-up hadn't helped hide the fatigue. *Oh, well.*

An unexpected sound caused her to jump. *Easily spooked these days, aren't you?* She shook her head at the large pile of mail on the floor under the mail slot. She read each return address and tossed them on the couch, plopping down beside the pile. Mail that read *Nadia Comings* still sent prickles through her. *What a day; what a week!* She settled her head against the back of the couch and tried to calm her rattled nerves by closing her eyes. Being on edge all the time could wear a person out. Her eyes hadn't been closed five minutes when her work phone rang.

"Hello, Caldwell and Associates, Ms. Lucas speaking, how can I help you?"

"You forgot a piece of mail, *Nadia*."

Click.

She flipped the phone shut and slowly turned her head toward the front door. A single white envelope lay on the floor. Trembling took over her body. Sweat moistened her palms and her breathing accelerated. She swallowed hard against her stomach as it protested keeping the recently-eaten lunch where it belonged. She walked across the room to the bay window and separated two blind slats just enough to see through.

Nothing.

She lowered herself onto the cushioned seat and sat motionless. Not sure how much time had passed, Nadia focused on the clock that hung next to her door.

Two forty-five. Trent doesn't get off work until five, plus he said he had things to do before coming over. What do I do now?

She walked over and picked up her work phone. She dialed Jenny's private number. It rang three times before she answered. "Hello?"

"Hi, Jenny, it's Nadia. I'm sorry to call you on your cell at work, but I need you to do me a favor."

"Ms. Lucas, you sound upset."

"Everything is fine, but will you please have Mr. Macalister call me when he gets out of his meeting? I don't want to interrupt him in the middle of it. Please, Jenny, don't forget."

"I'll catch him as soon as he comes out," Jenny reassured her.

Flipping her phone shut, she set it down next to her. Minutes passed before she walked over to where the white envelope lay. She bent over and picked it up. Trembling hands flipped it over, searching it for a clue as to who had sent it. There was no writing anywhere. She walked into her office, pulled open the desk drawer and picked up the letter opener. She inserted it in the tiny crinkled edge and pulled it all the way across the top, then looked inside.

This was *not* empty.

She pulled out a piece of notebook paper and

unfolded it. She read each of the three words aloud.

"Almost time, Nadia."

Every muscle in her body tightened at once. The paper fell from her fingers and slowly drifted to floor beside her. She blinked and set the tears free. They rolled steadily down her cheeks as she collapsed into the chair.

"Who is doing this? Surely it's not -- ?" She could not bring herself to think about that awful night. "No, it can't be."

The memory overtook her.

Eric walked in the back door after putting up the mower. "It sure is hot out there today."

"You're right. Do you think we should cancel the cook out?" Nadia looked up from her store list.

"Nah, it'll be cooler when the sun goes down, hopefully." Eric chuckled.

"Yes, hopefully! I don't care for it when it's this hot out. Maybe we should think about getting a pool."

"I think that's a great idea. You should call tomorrow and find out all the details."

"Will do, honey. But for now I'm headed to the store. Look over the list and make sure I have everything we need, while I get my shoes on." She handed him the list before starting up the stairs.

"Will do."

Nadia rubbed her temples, breathing out a sigh of relief as the pounding faded away. She rested her head in her hands.

"Lord, give me wisdom, grace, protection, and peace. Help me to figure out who is doing this and why."

A dulled ringing sound caught her attention. Running to the living room, she grabbed her phone.

"Hello!"

"Nadia, it's Trent. You're out of breath. What's wrong?"

"I ran to answer the phone. It was on the couch. I was in my office. I didn't want to miss your call."

"Jenny told me to call you. I just got out of the meeting. What do you need?"

"I was just wondering if you knew what time you would be over?" She tried to control the emotion in her voice but it did not work.

"I have a couple quick things I have to finish up. I'll go ahead and take off after that, and get my errands done tomorrow. So I should be there in about forty-five minutes. Is that ok?"

"Yes, Trent, that's fine. Thank you." She quickly flipped the phone shut before he could ask anything else. *This is not like me.*

Lungs crying for air, she finally remembered to breathe. Forty- five minutes was a lot easier to deal with than three to four hours.

Chapter 4

Nadia kept busy straightening up her office, going through the mail...*again,* and taking a shower. She forced herself not to look at the clock every couple of minutes. She gripped the armrests of the kitchen chair when she heard a knock at the door. Her eyes glanced up at the time and her body relaxed.

A sudden feeling of flip-flops hit her stomach, replacing the almost constant twisting of fear. Trying to ignore it but unable to avoid feeling grateful, she forced her lips into a smile as she opened the door. "Hi, Trent. Please, come on in."

"Thanks. Nice place you have here."

"Thank you. Can I get you anything?"

"No, I'm fine, but are you?"

"Of course I am. You're here with me now." *Great. Where did that come from?*

Trent's head tilted. His eyebrows raised as a smile crossed his face. "Shall we sit and talk?" He gestured toward the couch.

"Sure, what would you like to talk about?"

"How about you tell me everything that's going on, starting with why you called to see what time I'd be over. Did something else happen?"

I am so not ready to do this. Where do I even begin? I can't tell him everything. What if he never wants to see me again?

Nadia fought off her fear with a prayer and

explained about the letter dropped in her mail slot.

"It makes me sick to my stomach to even think about it," she concluded. What was the point in trying to hide her fear?

Silence filled the air between them. Her heart raced as she sat waiting for him to respond, picking at her nails. Patience was *not* her strong point.

Finally he spoke. The velvety voice she had been waiting for still caused her to jump.

"What are you not telling me? I know there has to be more to this." *Why does that look of his ... so strong, so serious ... break my heart?*

I can't do this. I can't bring him into the middle of everything, especially when I don't even know what 'everything' is! And how does he see through me so easily? Am I really that transparent? Great.

"Look, Trent, I'm fine. I shouldn't have called you in the first place. I don't know why I'm even letting it get to me. I'm just being silly."

Maybe she could convince him, if not herself.

"Nadia, I know you like to put your game face on and make everyone think you are perfectly fine. I've seen you do it several times at work. But, the fact is, this is really upsetting you for some reason, and you chose me to reach out to. That tells me you trust me on some level. I'm just sorry you don't... I don't know... trust me enough to tell me everything. I wish you would. At least maybe I'd better understand why all this is happening in the first place, and actually be able to help you."

A soft whisper broke through her barely-parted lips. "I do trust you. I don't want to. I don't even like it, but I do."

"I'll be here whenever you're ready."

The gentle squeeze on her hand broke through the final wall that surrounded her heart. She inhaled a deep breath, closed her eyes and rolled her shoulders.

He waited.

"I was in college, studying for my finals at the library. A guy sat down next to me. He struck up a conversation, and we just hit it off. We were with each other almost every day after that. We fell in love and got married a few months later. I had never been so happy in my life. His name was... Eric Comings."

Confusion mixed with a tinge of sadness swept over his face.

"Go on."

"It was the middle of summer. We had been married exactly two weeks and we had made plans to have a bunch of friends over for a celebration of sorts. I headed out to the store to pick up the last-minute things we needed, while he picked up around the house."

Nadia closed her eyes against that one paralyzing memory she had to bring to the surface.

Her voice cracked. "We didn't have our get-together that night." Tears rolled freely down her cheeks.

"When I came home, I called out for Eric to help me put the groceries up. He didn't answer. He *always* answered. I called out his name louder, hoping he just hadn't heard me. Still nothing. I ran outside looking for him. He wasn't there. I ran upstairs." Her shoulders slumped as she leaned back on the couch. "I found him lying on our bed. I ran over to him, shaking him, calling out his name. He never moved; never answered me."

"What happened?"

"The autopsy said he was poisoned." She wiped the tears from her face. "Two days after his funeral I received a letter in the mail. No return address, no name. Just like the one today. Only difference was what it said."

"What did the first letter say?"

She tried to control her shaky voice enough for him to understand her. It wasn't easy.

"It said, *I'm coming, Nadia.*"

She watched his chest rise fast and then release the air slowly. He was clearly working up the nerve to ask his next question.

"And the one today; what did it say?"

"*Almost time, Nadia.*" She swallowed hard, watching Trent, waiting for his reply. She fiddled with a loose thread on her sleeve. *What is he thinking? That he'd be smart to run out the door and never come back, I bet.*

They both sat motionless for only a minute, and then suddenly she found herself wrapped up in his arms. *So this is what safety feels like?* She buried her head in his shoulder and released the built-up pain, hurt, and anger. Through her uncontrollable sobs, she heard some of the prayer he whispered for her.

"Do you have any family or friends here you could stay a night or two with?" he finally asked in a soft, calm voice.

"I don't have any family living. There's my friend Mindy. She's a real estate agent. I know she's been really busy lately, so I would hate to bother her. Besides, I don't want to get her involved in whatever this is."

"That's probably smart thinking. I want you to get

a few changes of clothes, and anything else you need for a couple days away. I know of a great place we can go to this weekend. But first we need to call the police and let them know what's going on."

"I can't run from this anymore, Trent. I've been doing that since Eric died. It's getting me nowhere. Whoever it is doing this, will find me, just like they did this time."

"Well, it still won't hurt to put a little distance between us and them, right? Besides, I'm not going to walk away and pretend everything is just fine, especially with all that you just told me. So, go get some things." He looked down at his watch. "We'll just stop by the police station on the way to my apartment. I'll need to pick up a couple of things as well.

"All right, I'll go pack some things and be out in a few minutes." She pushed herself up from the couch and made her way to the bedroom. She stood facing her bed, a million thoughts running through her mind, all jumbled together, none of them making sense; none of them staying in reach of her mind's grasp.

She pulled out a suitcase from under the bed and began filling it.

Lord, please protect us from harm. You are my strength and hope. My faith is in you. I know you are in control of every part of my life. Fill me with courage and boldness as I face my future.

Chapter 5

Looking up after zipping her suitcase, Nadia caught her reflection in the mirror above her dresser. That unsettled expression was starting to seem normal.

She plopped down on the bed and let herself fall back. Staring up at the ceiling, she realized she had never noticed all the tiny grooves and swirls. *So many things taken for granted. Lord, help me not take anything else for granted ever again. No matter how small it may seem.*

A dull thump filled the room. She heard Trent clear his throat through the door panel. "Are you ready?"

"Yes, I think so." She got up and grabbed her suitcase. "You can come in."

Trent walked over to her and gently kissed her head. "Everything is going to work out, Nadia. Come on." He reached out his hand.

She wasn't so sure. How could he be?

"Do you need anything else?"

She shook her head as she walked over to pick up her keys. After taking one last look around, she pulled the door closed behind them and locked it.

Trent placed her luggage in the back of his Chevy Silverado and then opened the door. She climbed in as he circled the truck to the driver side. The engine roared to life.

"Are we still stopping by the police station first?"

"Yep, sure are."

"I don't know if I can do it. I mean, I don't know if I can tell the whole story again. It's painful." She looked away, not wanting to see his reaction. "I moved from Pine Ridge so I wouldn't have to face this and so I could get on with my life. I'm…I guess I'm just scared. I don't want to run anymore though." Her hands covered her face as she steadied her nerves.

"I know, but I'll be right there with you. All you have to do is tell them exactly what you told me."

"You make it sound so easy."

"I'm sorry. I'm not meaning to. I know it's hard for you. But you're a strong woman. I have faith that you can do what needs to be done."

Nadia went through several scenarios in her mind. She rehearsed what she would say and imagined the officer's response, until finally, she convinced herself that what Trent had said was true.

"You're right, Trent. I can and will do this, with God's help."

Trent put the truck in park and turned off the key. "Ready?"

"I guess."

He pulled open the door to the police station. Nadia took in the way the place made her feel, the smells, the little cubicles lining the outside walls on both sides. Finally, she rested her eyes on the big reception desk in the middle of the newly-polished wooden floor. She walked up to the window and smiled at the woman sitting behind the desk.

"How can I help you?"

The warm, comforting, hand on her back gave her the extra bit of courage she needed.

"Yes, I need to speak with a detective, please."

"Mick Warren is our detective, ma'am, but he's not in right now. Here is his card. You can call him after you've spoken to one of the regular officers. If you'll have a seat I'll have someone meet with you in just a few minutes."

Nadia took the card from the friendly receptionist and placed it in her purse and walked over to the chairs by the big glass door. Shortly, an officer appeared and led them back to his cubicle. "I'm Officer Todd Mitchell." She shook his outstretched hand and introduced herself and Trent.

"It's nice to meet you. Please sit down. I hear you want to talk with Detective Warren." He pulled out a file and laid a pad of paper on the desk in front of him. "Who wants to tell me what's going on?"

Nadia faced Trent, whispered a prayer, turned back to face the officer and began her story.

"That went well, don't you think?"

Nadia rolled her eyes. "I guess. It wasn't as bad as I thought it was going to be, at least."

"I knew you could do it."

Would she ever get used to the feeling in her gut when he smiled at her? Probably not, but she wanted to try.

"It'll take me a few minutes to get my things together, so if you want, you can give Detective Warren a call at my place while you wait."

"That sounds good."

"In the meantime, are you hungry? I can stop and

pick us up something. I'm afraid I don't keep much food in my bachelor pad." He winked.

"I am getting a little hungry. I can pay for my own." She got out a ten-dollar bill and placed it in the cupholder between them.

Trent shook his head. "I'm not letting you pay for anything, so put that money back in your purse."

Nadia started to protest, but instead picked up the money and placed it back in her wallet.

Trent smiled. "Good, now what would you like to eat?"

"I guess a burger and fries."

"All right, burger and fries it is."

Chapter 6

Nadia waited behind Trent, hands full of takeout bags and drinks.

"Find the right key yet? This is getting pretty heavy you know." Teasing him was something she didn't get to do often. She enjoyed it, not to mention it helped take her mind off the circumstances.

He laughed. "Rub it in while you can."

It took a moment for her eyes to adjust when the light snapped on in front of her.

"Follow me." Once they reached the kitchen, Trent set the drinks on the table. She followed suit with the bags of food and then sat down across from him. They held hands and bowed their heads as he said grace.

"So where are we headed to?" Nadia asked between bites.

"It's just a little place my uncle owns up in Lake Hills."

"Little place, huh? Does this little place have a name?"

"Of course."

"Are you going to tell me?"

"It's called The Blue Lake Hotel."

"I'm guessing it's by a lake?"

Trent grinned. "Yes it's by a lake; a very blue one."

When they had finished, Nadia gathered the bags

and napkins off the table, tossing them in the trashcan. She reached in her pocket for her phone, but all she felt was soft material.

"Um, Trent," she called down the hallway.

"Yeah."

"I left my phone out in your truck."

"Okay, hold on and I'll walk out with you. I'm pretty sure I locked it."

"Okay."

Nadia scratched her head as a frown formed on her lips. "I thought maybe it would be in the seat. But it's not there. It's not in the cupholder either." She pushed her arm between the seat and the console. "I can't find it anywhere."

"Hold on a second; I'll call it."

She listened intently for any faint ringing sound. "I think I hear it." She grabbed her suitcase. "I know I didn't put it in here."

"I don't remember you putting it in there either."

Nadia picked up the suitcase. "Will you call it again please?"

"Sure."

"I hear it." She unfolded a shirt and grabbed her phone. Underneath it was a plain white envelope. Staring, heart pounding, she froze.

Her phone rang out and sent a slight vibration up her arm. "Hello?"

"Hello, Ms. Lucas?" A strange, gruff voice coming through the phone caught her by surprise. "This is Detective Warren. I received your paperwork from Officer Mitchell. I'm free tonight at eight; does that work for you?"

Nadia looked at her watch. *Thirty minutes.* "Yes,

eight tonight is fine."

"Great, we'll meet at the police station. Please bring those letters and envelopes with you if you have them."

"Yes, I have them. I'll bring them, along with the latest one I just found."

"You've received another letter since the time you left the police station?"

"Yes, sir, about ten minutes ago."

"Have you opened it yet?"

"No, I just found it."

"Please don't open it or touch it any more than necessary. Bring it along with any others. I'll see you soon."

"He said not to open it, and be careful touching it." Trent nodded, rolled the phone and the letter up in the shirt, and handed them back to Nadia. She lifted her hand to her head, and rubbed at the nagging throb. Tears streamed down her face. "This is crazy."

"At least the detective has time to meet with us tonight. Speaking of which, we should really get going. Let me grab my things and we'll get out of here."

Nadia rolled the soft material of her blouse back and forth between her fingers. She arched her back, easing the discomfort from the hard plastic chair. The uncomfortable feeling of being watched sent a chill down her spine. She turned. A lifeless stare held her captive, even though the blue eyes were barley visible behind long blonde hair.

"Ms. Lucas?"

She jerked. "Yes."

"Hi, I'm Detective Warren." The newcomer reached out his hand.

"Nice to meet you, Detective."

"Who is the gentleman with you today?"

"His name is Trent Macalister, sir; he's a good friend of mine from work."

He signaled them to follow.

"Here we are. Please make yourselves comfortable." He pointed to the dark, red- cushioned chairs in front of his desk.

"I've looked over the report you filled out earlier. However, please go ahead and start from the very beginning for me, Ms. Lucas."

She took a deep breath and began. The detective scribbled notes on the pad of paper in front of him; only interrupting occasionally to ask a question. When she was finished, he laid down his pen and sat quietly for a minute, rubbing his chin.

"Did you bring the envelopes with you, Ms. Lucas?"

"Yes, sir." She unrolled the shirt, got the other one from her purse, and placed them on the desk.

"Great. Hopefully we can get some kind of prints off these. Now, has anyone else touched these besides you?"

"Trent has."

"I'll get both of your fingerprints so we can have those for elimination. I'll be right back."

She looked at Trent. He patted her knee. "It's just a sample, Nadia. That way they know ours from anyone else's. It's fine. Just remember, God's in control."

"I know. Just wish it felt more like it." She glanced

at the floor. "I wish I knew the meaning behind all of this."

The vibrations from Detective Warren's heavy foot steps announced his return. He placed a box on his desk. "Here are the fingerprint kits. Please do each finger on both hands. Then you can wash up and we'll be finished here." He cleared his throat and continued. "Ms. Lucas, I would recommend you stay with someone this weekend, maybe even for the next week or so."

"I'll be with Trent this weekend. We're staying at his uncle's hotel. It's about an hour away. Is that okay?"

"Yes, of course. That's probably a good idea."

After rolling each moistened finger in the small boxes on the card, Nadia wiped off on the damp towel the detective had placed on his desk. Her eyes met Trent's and a slight smile crossed her face. "Your turn."

She watched as the detective picked up the cards and placed them in the file.

"I've got your number, Ms. Lucas, so whenever I find out something, I'll give you a call."

"Thanks, Detective Warren. I'll have my phone close by at all times."

"Don't hesitate to call if something else happens, no matter how small you may think it is."

"I will. Thank you."

Nadia walked out of the police station. Her eyes focused on the pebbly walk retreating beneath her feet. She felt a searing in her soul and stopped in her tracks. She turned and was met again by the lifeless blue-eyed stare.

"What are you looking at?"

She saw Trent looking in the same direction she had been only seconds ago. She looked back. The man was gone. "Nothing." She said as she made her way to the truck.

"I don't believe you. Come on, get in and tell me."

"I'm probably just making too much of things," she said, shutting the truck door.

"So, tell me anyway."

"Did you see that man sitting across from us in the waiting room?"

"Yes, I remember him. What about him?"

"I think he was watching us from across the road just now."

"Do you know him?"

"I don't know."

"What does that mean, you don't know?"

She saw the questioning look in his eyes.

"I'm not sure." She shrugged. "He looked vaguely familiar, but his eyes….his eyes remind me of… Eric's."

"*Eric?*"

"I know it sounds crazy. That's why I didn't want to say anything. I'm pretty sure it was the same guy I saw at the café while we were having lunch."

"Obviously you're not crazy. It confirms our need to get out of town for awhile, or however long it takes. Let's go back in and let the detective know about this guy."

Beep! Beep! Beep!

"What's going on?" Nadia turned and looked out

the back window at the car behind them.

"I don't know. Maybe I'm going too slow."

"Too slow? You're going the speed limit. How fast do they want you to go?"

Nadia flung forward with the force of the car hitting their rear bumper. The squelch of metal grated against her ears.

"Trent! What's going on?"

"I don't know. Are you ok?"

"Yes I'm fine. Just please get us away from this person!"

"I'm trying, Nadia. Hold on."

Her eyes darted to Trent's foot as he jammed the gas pedal to the floor. She grabbed the handle above the door and prayed.

"Can you get to your phone?"

"Yes."

"Call Detective Warren!"

Nadia dialed the numbers as fast as she could. "Great, voicemail."

She hung up after leaving a message and turned to face Trent. "Have we lost them?"

"I think so.

"What do we do now?"

"I guess wait for the detective to call you back and pray they don't find us again."

Guilt gripped her heart. "I'm sorry."

"You don't have anything to be sorry about, Nadia."

"If only I hadn't called you today."

"Don't talk like that."

"It's the way I feel."

"Well, stop it. I want to be here for you. I know

I'm *meant* to be here for you. Anyway, we'll talk more when we get to the hotel."

Nadia sat in silence as she watched the buildings pass by out the window. *How can life change so much in such a short amount a time? Will things ever be normal again?*

"So." She broke the silence. "Have you ever lived up this way?"

"Yes, I have," he smiled. "I use to live about ten minutes from here eight years ago. Lake Hill is a nice, quiet town. I miss living here sometimes. But, if I had never moved to Harvest Hills…" Redness flushed his cheeks. "I wouldn't have met you."

Nadia turned her head, hiding her own flushed cheeks and smile. *What exactly did he mean by that?* "No, I guess you wouldn't have."

"Our rooms are right next to each other."

"That makes me feel better."

"I thought it would. I know you."

"That's both terrifying and comforting."

He laughed. "Don't be terrified. I'm on your side, remember?"

"Still, it's a little strange. No one has ever known me that well – not even Eric."

Trent sighed. "Maybe that's because you never let your guard down enough for people to know you."

"And that's a bad thing?"

"It can be. You have to learn to trust some people, Nadia, or you'll be a very lonely person."

"True, I guess."

"I'm thankful you've let me in."

"I am, too."

"So, what do you think?" He pulled into the hotel parking lot. "Nice enough for you?"

Nadia sat with her mouth open for a moment. The two-story brick building sat among thick shrubbery and beds of purple arctic phlox. A small circular window was set above the breezeway that reached out over the drop-off. Long, rectangular windows lined the first and second floors, giving each room a picture-perfect view of the trees and wild flowers that filled the landscape. "I'd say so! It's *beautiful.*"

"Wait until you see the inside." Trent got the bags out of the back of the truck.

"How long has your uncle owned this place?"

"Ever since he built it, ten years ago."

"He *built* it?"

"Well, he *had* it built, I guess I should say."

Nadia walked through the double glass doors and stopped. Her jaw dropped as her eyes took in the scene before her.

Three columns lined each side of the entrance leading to a wide staircase. A desk sat in the middle of the lobby floor with an attractive, middle-aged woman behind it with the check-in computer off to her right. The brown-carpeted staircase directly behind her rose to a landing before splitting off to the left and right with a couple of steps that led to the second floor. Chandeliers hung every few feet in the upstairs hallways.

Wow!

"Hello, Mr. Macalister. Your rooms are ready. Take the stairs, turn right, and you're in the first two rooms."

"Thank you, Ms. White."

"Let me call someone to get your things."

"That's not necessary. I've got it. Thanks, though."

"I don't believe Mr. Clark would be happy with me if I let you carry your things."

"I promise you won't have any trouble from my uncle."

Trent turned to Nadia. "Are you ready to go to your room?"

Nadia smiled as she passed the woman behind the desk. She walked quickly to catch up with Trent. "I can't *believe* this place. Everything is so pretty. That light blue shade on the walls is so perfect. It contrasts so nicely with the dark brown of the carpet."

"My uncle spared no expense in making sure it looked nice. He wanted people to have a 'fancy' place to come to without having to go far or spending a fortune."

"I'd say he accomplished that!"

"I'll let him know you approve." He smiled and reached out his hand. "Here's the key to your room. Remember, I'm right next door. If you need anything, call my cell or the room. Just dial 201. Hey speaking of cell, did Detective Warren ever call you back?"

"I haven't heard my phone ring, but I'll check in a minute, after I get my stuff inside."

"Get settled in. I will be over in about ten minutes. We can check your phone then. If he hasn't called, we'll try him again."

"Okay."

Her anticipation grew as she unlocked the door. *If*

downstairs is that pretty, what will I find behind this door? She pushed the door open and flipped on the lights. She shook her head in disbelief. *He definitely didn't spare any expense. I wonder what it costs to stay here?*

The room was much bigger than a normal hotel room, but had a warm and cozy feel about it. White, crisp sheets and a light-blue blanket covered the four-poster bed that sat almost in the middle of the room on a raised gray platform with three steps leading up each side.

A black desk painted with silver flowers sat off to the right. Next to it was a huge window covered by dark blue curtains that hung to the floor. A flatscreen TV hung on the wall over a fireplace, in direct line with the bed.

She opened the double oak doors next to the TV to find a sunken bathtub right in the middle of the floor. To the left was a shower, and to the right were double sinks and a toilet. The pale blue wallpaper with light silvery swirls that covered the bedroom walls flowed seamlessly into the bathroom.

A soft knocking roused her as she turned back toward her suitcase. *Had it been ten minutes already?*

She turned the knob and opened the door. Trent smiled.

"Come on in."

"Thank you."

"I haven't checked my phone yet. I've been in awe of the room."

"Glad you approve."

"Wise move, Mr. Macalister. Very wise move."

"Do you know where your phone is offhand? I can

check it for you."

She pointed to the bed. "It's in the side pocket of my purse."

"I found it. Looks like you missed a call." He held the phone out to her.

Chapter 7

Her mind went blank. Hard plastic hit the top of her foot. She didn't feel it.

"Nadia, what's wrong?" Trent placed his hands on her shoulders, gently shaking her. "Nadia?" He wasn't getting anywhere. He bent down, picked up the phone, and put it to his ear. *To replay the message, please press one now.* He put the phone back to his ear.

"Ms. Lucas! This is Jenny. Where are you? Your house is on fire. Please answer. I have to know you're not in there! Ms. Lucas!"

Nadia blinked several times before shaking her head from side to side. A sense of comfort flowed through her from the two strong hands that again rested on her shoulders.

"Nadia, you need to call Jenny back and let her know you're all right."

She drew strength from his steady gaze and nodded. "I know. I will. I just need to sit down for a few minutes first."

She reached out her hand, palm up, and waited for him to place the phone in her hand. *This can't really be happening, can it?*

Her eyes remained focused on the phone for several minutes before she dialed Jenny's number, trying to wrap her head around the message she had heard.

"Nadia -- I mean, Ms. Lucas -- is that you? Are you okay?" The urgency in Jenny's voice brought the severity of it all to life.

Nadia's response barely made it past her throat. "Yes, Jenny. I'm okay. I wasn't there. I just now got your message."

"I'm so glad you're not hurt. I was so worried. I had just driven off from putting the files in your mail slot. I wasn't two minutes away when I looked back and saw smoke, so I turned around and called 911. I was so scared when I realized it was *your* house. The firefighters are here now, and the police. There was a Detective Warren looking for you. I wasn't able to help him since I don't know where you are."

"I'm safe. That's what matters. I will call Detective Warren in a couple minutes. Did they say if they know what happened?" Her voice cracked. "How the fire started?"

"No, not yet. Where are you? I can come and get you. You shouldn't be alone right now."

"I'm not alone. Trent is with me."

"Are you sure? I don't mind. You know I'll do anything I can to help you."

"I appreciate that. I'll call you back later. Thanks, Jenny." She flipped her phone shut and set it down beside her.

"Come sit down." Trent patted the empty couch cushion next to him. "I called Detective Warren while you were on the phone with Jenny. I let him know we are safe and where we are. I also filled him in on the guy at the police station, and whoever chased us out of town. He wants us to stay put for now. He said he was able to talk with some of your neighbors." Nadia raised her head when he didn't continue speaking. She walked over and sat next to him. "Go on."

"Well, they -- your neighbors that is -- all said the same thing."

"Which was?"

"They saw a woman at your door minutes before the fire started."

"The woman was Jenny. She told me that she had just left after dropping off my files. I forgot to bring them with me at lunch today, remember?

Anyway, when she looked in her rearview mirror she saw smoke and turned around. She called 911 and waited for the police to get there."

She could sense Trent's uneasiness. "What's wrong?"

"Nadia, I don't know how to tell you this, but from what your neighbors said, Jenny never left after dropping off your files. She went back to her car, but never drove away. A lady saw smoke a couple minutes later and called 911."

She tilted her head, a look of disbelief on her face. "Are you saying Jenny lied? That she's *in* on this?"

"All I know is what the detective told me. I hope she isn't, though."

Nadia's thoughts raced, trying to place all the pieces together like a puzzle in her mind. "She told me *she* called 911. This is crazy! Why would Jenny do something like this?"

Trent shook his head. "I wish I could tell you Nadia; but I honestly don't know."

"She was trying to find out where I was, too. She kept saying she'd come and get me."

"Did you tell her?"

"No. I just told her that I was safe and with you. She said she talked to the detective too. Maybe we should ask him to keep an eye on her?"

"Good idea, Nadia. I'll call him back right now."

She didn't notice when Trent hung up, until she heard him calling her name from what seemed like miles away.

"Nadia." Trent's gentle voice broke through, her eyes now clearly focused on his. "He said he would keep an eye on her. However, there's something else I think you should know."

"What?"

"An older couple a few doors down from you said they saw a man standing on the sidewalk watching the fire, which they thought was no big deal, at first anyway, until they overheard him on the phone saying, 'Why did you set the house on fire?' They said he was upset. They described him as tall, with long blond hair."

She pushed down the lump in her throat. "So Jenny *knows* him? *How?*" She was not able to hold the tears back any longer. Her head sank.

"She didn't know I was going to the police station, though. *I* didn't even know! So how did he?"

"There are a lot of questions that need answers, but I'm not sure when or how we will get them. God will continue to guide us, Nadia. He has so far, right? He protected us from whoever was chasing us today. He made it so that you were over an hour away from your home when it caught on fire. It's all God's hand on your life...on *our* lives."

"I know. It's just hard, you know? To hold onto your faith sometimes, especially when things like this are happening."

"If life was always easy, we wouldn't need to *have*

faith, would we?"

"No, I guess we wouldn't."

"We can trust God to always be truthful, right?"

"Right."

"He says he'll never leave us or forsake us correct?"

She smiled. "Correct."

"So, that means that even in this scary time we can trust that He's here...*with us.*"

His words sank into her spirit. "You're right. I know God is with us. It just seems so easy for you, though. Maybe you're more grounded in your faith than I am."

"I don't know that I would say that. I gave my heart to the Lord several years ago, but that doesn't mean I haven't come up against hard times and had to learn a thing or two. But I look back and see God's guidance and deliverance. I trust that he'll bring me through the next one, as long as I hold on."

"From the way you talked at lunch, I thought you'd always been saved."

She watched with questioning eyes as Trent bit his lip. "Trying to keep from laughing, are you?"

"That's exactly what I'm trying to do," he chuckled. "My dear, Nadia, there's so much you don't know about me."

"Great. Should I be worried?"

"No, not at all, although you might be a little surprised."

"Ummm, that may be true, but I still don't think it can be anything too bad."

Trent focused his eyes on the fireplace. "I wish I could say that's true, Nadia. Unfortunately, I can't.

That story is for another time. I will tell you though, that the Lord found me and brought me out of a screwed-up mess I had gotten myself into." His eyes met hers. "Let's just say this isn't the first time my life's been in danger. Like I said, though, that's another story, and one that's not important right now. What is important is that we both get some sleep."

"That's not nice. You tell me something like that and then tell me to go to bed?" She rested her hands on her hips, before letting them gently fall to her sides. "It's not like I'm going to be able to sleep anyway." She whispered.

"You should at least try."

Her shoulders relaxed as she exhaled. "I will."

"I'm going to go. If you need me call."

"Goodnight."

"Goodnight, Nadia."

"Trent."

"Yes?"

"Thank you."

"You're welcome."

Chapter 8

After much tossing and turning, Nadia tried commanding her body to rest, but it would not listen. She threw the covers back and sat up. Her legs dangled over the side of the bed. She made her way through the double oak doors, grabbed a towel, and turned on the faucet. She let it run for a few minutes before she undressed and slowly lowered herself into the warm water. *Maybe all I need is a nice warm bath to calm me down.*

Her eyes closed as she rested her head on the back of the tub.

Dear Lord, I'm so confused. My mind cannot find peace. I feel like I'm going to burst. Even though it's hard for me to understand, and hard for me to keep my faith in this crazy time, I'm going to keep believing. Forgive me for my doubts and fill me with your peace and guidance. Surround Trent and me with your protection. Give Detective Warren and the police the wisdom to figure out this case. Lead our footsteps so that we are never out of your will and surround us with you peace.

She sat awhile longer, enjoying the warmth, before pulling the plug and wrapping a robe around her. Standing mesmerized, she watched the water as it disappeared. The swirling and slight gurgle made the perfect rhythm to ease her mind, making way for a long-lost memory to resurface…

"Come on Nadia, just jump in. I'm right here. I won't let you get hurt."

"I don't know, Eric. I'm not big on swimming. You know that."

Everyone cheered her on. "You can do it, Nadia!"

Smiling, Eric reached his arms out toward her. "I'll catch you."

"Oh, all right."

The water trickled down her face as she came to the surface. "That was so much fun!"

"See, I told you that you'd like it. You just have to trust me." Eric laughed.

"Yeah, trust him!"

Nadia turned at the high-pitched squeal behind her. "You must be Lily. I'm so glad you made it. Eric's told me so much about you, I feel like we're already friends."

"Aww. How sweet!" Lily laughed as she pulled her strawberry-blonde hair from her ponytail and jumped in the pool with them. "I think we'll be good friends. Us girls have to stick together, right?"

Lily…her eyes and petite stature brought another person to mind. "Jenny… is *Lily?*"

She dressed quickly and picked up her cell from the table. Pacing back and forth, she waited for Trent to answer.

"Hello?" A groggy voice answered.

"Trent I've figured out how Jenny's involved!"

"Give me a few minutes and I'll be over."

"Please hurry!"

"I will."

Trent stared into Nadia's eyes. She was sure he could see the betrayal surfacing behind the confusion.

"I couldn't sleep so I took a bath, hoping it would help me relax. After getting out, I stood and watched as the water swirled down the drain. A memory came back to me. Eric and I were at a friend's pool party one night. Eric was in the water, trying to get me to jump in. I was scared, though, so it took him awhile to convince me; but finally I gave in and jumped. When I came up everyone was cheering, and Lily, a girl Eric had told me he was going to introduce me to, was waving at me. It was kind of strange, because I liked her right away, even though I only saw her that one time. I remember asking Eric about who she was. He said she was an old friend from back home; never anything more, so I just let it go. That probably was not such a good idea on my part. But anyway, when Jenny started working for me, I thought she looked vaguely familiar; one of those people you know you've seen before but can't remember where things. Well, I figured out where. It was at our friend's pool party. Lily is *Jenny,* Trent. Her hair's redder now, and she wears her make-up different, but it's her!"

"Are you sure?"

She nodded. "Yes, I'm sure."

"Wow." Trent scratched his head. "I wasn't expecting that."

"Do you think she knows who I am and that's why she started working for me?"

"I don't know…maybe. What time is it? I left my watch in my room."

"It's one-thirty."

"We've got some time before we can call Detective Warren, so let's do some brainstorming. Eric introduced her as a friend from back home, correct?"

"Yes."

"Where's he from?" Trent grabbed a pen and piece of paper from the desk drawer and sat back down.

"He was born in Indiana, but he didn't want to talk about his family. Do you think his parents are still alive? I just assumed he'd lost them."

"Guess we'll find out."

"I tried finding them after he died, just in case, but I didn't have any luck." A faint sigh escaped her. "I don't know if they know he's gone."

A strong hand squeezed hers as a tear flowed down her cheek. "Maybe Detective Warren will be able to find them."

"I hope so."

"Do you know of any other friends, or maybe some other family that could confirm Jenny is this Lily person?"

"No, not really. Eric only brought up his family one time, and all he told me then was his parents' names. After that, he said he never wanted to talk about them again, so I never brought it back up. And other than Lily, or Jenny, whatever her name is, I don't know of anyone he was friends with before he moved here."

"What are his parents' names?"

"His dad's name is Chester, and his mom's name is Molly."

"You said he moved here from Indiana? How long ago?"

"He said about two years before I met him."

"We'll give the detective their names. I'm sure he'll be able to find them. We'll also tell him what you remembered about Jenny."

Nadia shook her head. Knowing that somebody she had liked might be involved in all this somehow was hard to understand. A tiny spot of moisture dropped onto her jeans. "I guess things aren't ever what they seem."

"Don't cry, Nadia. We'll get this all figured out, somehow."

"I don't understand why they wanted us dead."

Trent tapped the pen against his leg as he stared off into space. Nadia joined in the silence and let her thoughts run free, hoping to come up with something. It was no use. Her brain was too tired to piece things together.

Chapter 9

Nick sat in his car, growing impatient, waiting for Lily to get home. He slammed his phone shut after leaving yet another message. Nothing was going according to plan and his temper was ready to explode. He punched the steering wheel. *Where are you, Lily?*

He heard a car pull up beside him. "Where have you been? I've been waiting for over an hour!" He slammed his car door shut and glanced at his watch. "Do you have an idea what time it is?"

"Yes, Nick, I know it's late."

"Late...you know it's late? Lily, it's two o'clock in the morning!"

"Please calm down and lower your voice. We don't want any more attention! Come on, let's go in." Lily fumbled through her purse until she found her keys. "I don't know why I never put the house keys on the same keychain as my car keys. It would make things a lot easier."

Nick pushed past her and stomped into the house. She calmly walked in behind him and shut the door.

"What are you thinking? Losing your cool out there for the whole neighborhood to see is not a smart move on your part, Nick. You have to maintain control if you want to finish this once and for all."

His glare sent a shiver through her.

"And just how are we going to finish this now? Everything is messed up, thanks to your little house fire. The plan will no longer work! Now the police are involved; not to mention this guy she's got hanging around. I thought you said they weren't even close?"

"Well, that's what she *said*. I guessed she had some kind of feelings for him, but I honestly never thought he'd take her off somewhere."

"I'll never be able to take over his life now."

"I knew it!"

Nick's icy blue stare cut right through her. "You knew *what?*" His voice was hard and empty.

"That you changed your mind. You want to take over Eric's life with *Nadia*, not with me."

A devilish grin appeared on his face; one Lily had never seen before.

"Now what makes you say that, Lily?"

"You said *I*, not *we*."

Nick sat down on the couch and rubbed his chin, softening his eyes as he stared at her. "Sorry, slight slip of the tongue in a moment of frustration. I meant *we*." He could still see the betrayal in her eyes. "Come over here next to me. Let's figure this out."

"Nick, you know I've always been there for you, playing whatever part you needed me to." She fell silent.

"Go on."

"Most of my life has been invested in you and your schemes, and I've always trusted you to work things out. I'm sorry I messed things up. I didn't mean to. I guess my jealousy finally got the best of me."

Nick placed his hand on her cheek. "What do you have to be jealous of? We've been together a long time, Lily. You are my other half in all this, right? Why would I want that to end? And besides, where would you get the idea that I want Nadia anyway?"

"I don't know," she sighed. "It's just a feeling."

"Well, we can't always trust our feelings now, can we?"

"No, I guess not."

"Do you remember what happened the last time someone let their feelings get in the way? He backed out, and almost cost us everything we'd worked for. So, I need to know you're with me on this. There's too much to lose."

He barely heard Lily's whispered words. "I'm with you, Nick."

"Good." He took her hands in his. "It's been a long hard day. Why don't you go take a nice, long, candlelight bubble bath? I'll bring you something to drink; something that will take your mind off everything."

"That sounds like a great idea. Are you sure you don't mind?"

"I'm sure. Go on now. I'll be there in a couple minutes. You go relax."

"Oh, Todd left a message for you on my phone. He said something about Lake Hills, but I couldn't really understand the rest of it."

"Okay." A sly grin spread across his face. "Maybe this will work out after all."

After watching Lily walk down the hall and into the bathroom, Nick made his way to the kitchen, took out a can of beer, and emptied it into a glass. "If you remember what happened to the last person who trusted their feelings, then darling, you shouldn't be so naïve to think the same thing wouldn't happen to you." He swirled the drink as he ambled down the hall to the bathroom. "Here you go," he said as he handed it to her. He glanced back and forth between her glass and the flickering candlelight dancing across the walls of the bathroom while he waited.

"Thank you, Nick. I really needed that."

He bent over and kissed her forehead. "I'm going to miss you, Lily. But I'll see you on the other side someday."

"What? What do you mean, you'll miss me? Nick, what are you talking about?"

He stared into her fear-filled eyes, watching as they slowly closed, then walked out, locking the door behind him as he dialed Todd Mitchell's number.

Chapter 10

Nadia prayed, paced, thought, and paced some more. The hours passed in slow motion as she and Trent talked. She tried gathering her thoughts into some kind of order. Her emotions swung from anger to sadness to confusion and then back through them all again like someone had hit a *repeat* button.

She glanced at the clock. In a few minutes, she'd be making the phone call to Detective Warren about what she had remembered and the ideas she and Trent had talked about throughout the night. Her stomach lurched. *All of this has to be a dream. It can't be real, can it?*

"That was a disappointing phone call." She looked at Trent. "No news. Not that I expected there to be, but I admit I had hoped."

The warmth of Trent's hand on hers brought a slight smile to her face.

"I vote we try and find the bright side of this situation."

Tilting her head to the side, she raised one eyebrow. "And the bright side of this situation would be … ?"

His now-familiar, slightly crooked smile melted her heart.

"Well, finding the bright side of something is all in how you look at it, right?"

She shrugged her shoulders. "I guess."

"So, let's think of something that makes the best of this bad situation."

"How do we do that, exactly?"

"I have an idea. There are two places I want to show you while we are here. Had this 'bad situation' never happened, who knows if you would have seen them?"

Nadia shook her head. "I guess anything to take my mind off this for awhile is worth it."

"How about we get some breakfast before we head out for a short walk? Be thinking about what you want while I go get cleaned up. I'll be back in about thirty minutes. The menu is over on the desk. Look it over and find something good." He winked, closing the door behind him.

Turning around, she faced the empty table. Puzzled, she pulled out the drawer. Her hand slid across the cool, smooth plastic. "There you are." Nothing on the menu caught her eye. "Eggs, bacon and toast will have to do." She picked up the phone and called the kitchen to place their order.

"Knock, knock," Trent said, entering the room.

"Wow, that was fast. I don't think it was a half hour though."

"I'm fast, what can I say? If you want though, I can leave and come back when it's been exactly thirty minutes."

She tried not to laugh as he walked to the door. "No, stay. I ordered our breakfast about ten minutes ago. It should be here soon."

"I like making you laugh. Thanks for ordering breakfast by the way." He smiled.

"You're welcome."

Trent grabbed the remote and plopped down on the gray couch located between the bed and the TV. "What would you like to watch this morning?"

"Whatever's on I guess. I hardly ever get to watch it. I don't even know what's on anymore."

He flipped through channels. "Looks like news, news, and more news."

"That sounds interesting." She rolled her eyes.

"I'm sure it will be." He patted the empty seat beside him. "Come sit next to me. You can help me figure out which station to watch." He turned to face her. "You look faint; are you ok?"

Raising her arm, she pointed toward the TV. "I think we need to watch this one."

The reporter stood in front of a blackened house frame with only one wall left standing. His lips moved, but Nadia didn't hear anything. *"That's my house. My car."*

Trent hurried to her side and cradled her in his arms. "Look at me, not that. We can't do anything to change that. We can, however, do something to change us; here, now, and in the future."

"What do you mean?"

"Room service," a voice outside the door called, and broke the tense moment between them.

"Coming."

The hotel employee pushed in the cart. "I'll be back for it in an hour. Enjoy your meal."

Trent gestured toward the food, "Let's eat. I'm sure it's much better hot than cold." He was met with silence.

Nadia inhaled deeply, walked around the couch and sat down. They held hands while he prayed. She forced herself to eat. Her movements were robotic. No flavor met her tongue, just the fleeting warmth and softness of the egg, and the crunch of the bacon.

Trent placed his fork on the empty plate. "Are you still up for our walk?"

Her heart warmed at his efforts to take her mind off everything. It would be rude to stay quiet and withdrawn. A forced smile tugged at her lips. "Sure. When?"

"We don't have to go, Nadia. I was just hoping you might have a little bit of fun, though."

Have fun! Is he serious? "Honestly Trent, it seems strange trying to have fun while so many things are going wrong. Of all the feelings running through me right now, fun is definitely *not* one of them."

"Maybe being out in nature will help ease the stress? You know, smelling the flowers, feeling the wind against your face. There's nothing strange about that, right?"

It did sound nice. "I'm glad I'm here with you."

"God leads us to the one we need, and the one who needs us."

"True."

Trent smiled. "Get your gym shoes on and whatever else you need. Don't forget your phone. I'll be waiting in the hall."

Chapter 11

"Come on." Trent grabbed Nadia's hand. You'll have fun, I promise." As hard as she tried she couldn't stay upset long around him.

"I better."

She locked the door and hurried to catch up with him. A warm sensation met her hand and climbed up her arm, until it filled her entire body. The corners of her mouth lifted. *Could this actually go somewhere?* She scolded herself for letting her mind wander in that direction. *You've got to get a grip!* She shook her head, willing the thought away.

Trent led her out the big glass doors, to the left, and around the building.

"That looks like a jungle, Trent."

"A jungle? Really? It's not a jungle; it's the woods. Big difference."

"Are you taking me in there?"

"That was the plan."

"What if we get lost?"

Trent shook his head. "You aren't the outdoors type, are you?" Not giving her time to respond, he added, "We won't get lost. You just walk a short distance and you come to a clearing. It's a very peaceful place."

She stopped as he stepped around in front of her.

"Do you trust me, Nadia?"

"Of course I trust you; it's the bugs and wild

animals in the woods I don't trust."

A tug dislodged her firmly planted feet. "You'll be sorry if you miss this."

An earthy smell filled her nose as they walked through a small clump of trees. Up ahead was the clearing. In it sat picnic tables, flowerpots, and a small play area off to the left. The canopy of leaves let streams of sunlight filter in here and there. Shadows danced when the wind blew.

"This is beautiful."

"I told you that you wouldn't want to miss it." A self-satisfied smirk made its way across his lips. Ignoring it, she walked over to a table and sat down. The warm breeze brushed her hair against her face and she pushed it behind her ear. A sweet fragrance filled the air. Their eyes locked.

"Nadia." A quiver touched his voice. "I know now is probably not the best time to do this. However, with all that is going on, it reminds me of how short life really is. The Bible even says we are not promised another day." He reached for her hand. "I've been praying for a long time for God to lead the woman he has chosen for me into my life. I knew that woman was you from the first time I saw you. I remember it so clearly. The wind blew your hair in your face as you were pulling open the door, walking into work. I tried to hurry and help you, but I didn't make it to you before you walked in."

He smiled. "It was the same day we ran into each other in the hallway. You know, I've seen you every Monday through Friday since then, and a couple times here and there on the weekends. Each moment spent with you only made my feelings stronger. Your smile, your laugh, the way you raise your eyebrow at me when I'm giving you a hard time, all those little things attract me to you even more." He paused. "I know we haven't known each other long, but I don't want to know what a day would be like without you in it." Her face sat cupped in his hands.

The warmth of the sun, the smell of the flowers, the light breeze, it was perfect. *Too perfect.* Her eyes closed and she felt his lips on her forehead. "I'm hoping you feel the same way about me, but if you don't, I understand."

Her heart pounded. Finally she gained the courage to speak. "You're right, Trent, there is a lot going on. It puts life into perspective a little more. Sad to think something as crazy as what we are facing makes us realize that." She felt a gentle squeeze on her hand. "The truth is…" *Why is this so hard?* "…the truth is, Trent, I have feelings for you too. I just don't know what to do with them yet." *There, I said it…finally.*

"You don't have to do anything with them. I know the last couple months have been hard for you. Just know I'm here when you're ready."

"Honestly, I wasn't expecting to meet anyone, let alone have feelings for someone so soon after Eric's death. It's a little confusing."

"More confusion is the last thing I want for you right now, but I had to let you know how I feel."

Nadia smiled and watched the flickers of sunshine dance in front of them. She stretched out her hands to soak up the warmth. "I'm glad you told me."

Hand-in-hand, they slowly walked back to the hotel. "I wish things could stay like this forever."

"Nadia, if life was always easy—"

She held up her hand. "I know, I know, we wouldn't need to trust in God, right?"

"Right."

She pulled her phone out of her pocket. Her forehead creased. "I wish Detective Warren would call with some news."

"It takes awhile to do some digging." Trent looked down at his watch. "It's been about five hours."

"Five hours is a long time when you're on the waiting end."

"What's that old saying?" He drummed his fingers on the desk.

"A watched pot never boils."

"Yeah, that's it."

"You are so funny."

"What do you say we get some lunch?"

"Geesh, I feel like all we do is eat."

"You need to do that to stay alive. Or am I wrong?"

Nadia turned toward the door. "I am not listening to you."

"I know, I know. Now which sounds better, grilled cheese, or a tuna sandwich?"

"I guess the grilled cheese."

"We can get something else."

"No, the grilled cheese does sound pretty good. I haven't had that in awhile."

Trent picked up the phone and called in their order. "It'll be up in about twenty minutes."

"So, how should we spend our last night in this amazing place?"

"I know that already."

"Okay. Care to fill me in?"

"After we eat some lunch I figured we could go to the store and pick up some things for a picnic."

"Are we going back where we were this morning?"

She watched as his smile took over his face. "No, I think you'll like this place better."

"I'll need some time to freshen up first."

"I figured."

After lunch Nadia's heart began to weigh heavily on the unknown future. Facing her reflection in the mirror was like a slap in the face. *How can Trent even stand to be seen with me? I look like such a mess right now.* She quickly touched up her make-up and brushed through her hair, tossing it up into a loose ponytail.

Nadia grabbed a blanket off the bed, wrapped it around her and sat down on the couch. She stared out into the stillness that surrounded her, concentrating on the good things in her life. A gentle knocking roused her from her thoughts.

"Nadia, it's me; are you ready?"

She tossed the blanket back on the bed, grabbed her keys and phone, and walked out the door. "Yep, I'm as ready as I'll ever be."

Nadia set the brand-new picnic basket on the small table in front of the couch. She ran her hand over the red-and-white checkered material that lined the inside and wrapped over the top. She had never been on a picnic before. Despite not being an outdoor person, excitement started overtaking her.

"Getting out of this room makes you that happy, huh?"

She giggled at Trent's wiggling eyebrows. "Yes, I guess it does. That and the fact I've never been on a picnic before."

"You've never been on a picnic, ever?" Trent tilted his head to the side.

"Not a real one. When I was little my mom and I use to have what we'd call indoor picnics."

"Those sound just as fun."

"They were. I miss those times."

"I think we can make your first 'outdoor picnic' just as fun."

"I'm sure we can."

Trent picked up the basket. "I'll get this if you'll get the blanket."

"I hate the thought of placing this new blanket on the dirty ground."

"It's the only one we could find, and I'm sure it won't mind."

Eyebrow up, lips pursed, Nadia was going to speak, but thought better of it.

"Follow me."

"I'm right behind you."

Nadia followed Trent down the stairs and out the front doors. After rounding the corner of the hotel, they walked for another ten minutes and came upon a huge boulder. They had just walked around it when she heard Trent speak.

"This is my uncle's favorite place. He hasn't told too many people about it."

In front of her was a grassy clearing filled with blue, white, and yellow wildflowers. A clear blue lake rippled and danced in the light of the sun. Off to the sides stood various kinds of trees, their leaves many different shapes and colors. *Mmmm, wildflowers; what a sweet smell.*

The blanket slipped from her hands as her jaw dropped. "The Lord knows how to paint such a beautiful scene."

"That he does." Trent agreed. "I thought you might like it." He picked up the blanket and took a few more steps forward before setting the basket down. He shook out the blanket and spread it across the ground before placing the basket on it, and went to stand beside Nadia.

"So, tell me what you think? Did I pick a good spot?"

"That's an understatement! This place is amazing. I'm torn between eating and just standing here soaking this all in. It couldn't get more beautiful than this."

"It's pretty in the winter. We can come back up then, if you like."

"Really?"

"Of course. Now can we please eat? My stomach thinks I forgot about it."

Once they were finished, Nadia packed the basket with the leftovers. She turned to Trent, face calm and serious. "Trent, through all of this you have been by my side. Honestly, it's a little shocking. Most guys, I think, wouldn't have even cared. Your friendship has meant the world to me over the last couple of months. I wasn't expecting to have feelings for someone ever again. I thought being that lucky only came around once in a lifetime. However, between the Lord and you, I've found that not to be true. So, I just wanted to thank you, again, for being here. You've made this all a little more bearable."

She searched his face as he sat silent. *Say something, please.*

"Nadia, I really believe that God has led us into each other's lives. He knows what he is doing; we just have to trust him. I'm grateful and honored to be by your side while you face – well – while you're facing this haunting from your past. Whatever you do, though, remember, you are not facing this alone. Even if I wasn't here with you, you wouldn't be alone. God is with you. He walks before you, guiding you on level paths, so you will not stumble and fall. He loves you, and because you love him, you can rest in his shadow, in his peace. He's your fortress, Nadia."

Trent looked around, pointing to the trees that encircled them. "God is your fortress. He's your peace. Just like this place we are sitting in right now. Beyond these trees is a noisy hotel and town. Who knew there was so much calmness and stillness in the midst of a bustling and hurried place? But we find this here, wrapped in the protection of tall shade trees, the cool breeze off the water, and the lingering smell of the wildflowers. If this is beautiful and peaceful to you, how much more so is God's peace?"

Nadia stood looking at all the beauty while letting what Trent had said sink in. "I'm going to call this *our place* from now on."

"*Our place.* I like that."

Chapter 12

Nadia pushed herself up from the couch and walked over to her suitcase, grabbing some pajamas before making her way to the bathroom. Her hand reached out to turn the water on just as her phone rang. She grabbed the robe from the hook and slipped it on before going to answer her phone. "Hello."

"Hello, Ms. Lucas, this is Detective Warren. I'm afraid I have some bad news." Nadia leaned her weight against the arm of the couch. "It concerns Lily Ryder."

She lowered herself down on the cushion, trying to brace her emotions for whatever news she was about to hear. "Go ahead."

"Ms. Lucas, Lily is dead. We found her in her home today. We're not sure what happened. There didn't appear to be a struggle of any kind, and there were no marks on her body. We'll know more soon."

Silence filled the line between them as Nadia fought back her tears. "I would check for some sort of poisoning," she whispered.

"We will."

"Thank you, Detective Warren. If there's nothing else, I really need to go now." Her voice cracked, giving away her emotions.

"There's nothing more, Ms. Lucas."

Nadia slowly flipped her phone shut and sat silent for a few moments before making her way back to the bathroom. She turned on the water and let her tears mix in with the drops running down her cheeks.

She ran her thumb over the smooth surface of the phone in her hand. It felt heavy. *Will this ever end?* She dialed Trent's number and waited. "Trent, Lily's dead." Her tongue was hardly able to form the words.

"I'll be right over, Nadia."

"You don't have to come over. I want to be alone. I just wanted to let you know."

"I understand. Promise you'll call if you need me?"

"I will."

Nadia lay in bed, staring at the back of her eyelids. *Lord, there are so many questions in this whole mess of things that just don't make sense. I know we aren't always supposed to understand everything, but it would be nice to know what's going on. Then again, maybe it wouldn't. I don't know, Lord. You know what's best. My faith is in you. Thank you for placing Trent in my life. The support he's shown me through all this has been amazing. I pray for our friendship to continue to grow. Guide our hearts and decisions. And please, Lord, let me get some much-needed rest tonight. You say in your word that when we lie down our sleep will be sweet. My mind and body need it. My soul needs it.*

Chapter 13

Startled awake, Nadia sat up and answered her phone. "Hello?"

"Good morning, Nadia, this is Detective Warren. Sorry to call you so early but I have some information I think you might want to know, and I'd prefer to tell you in person."

Great, that cannot be good. "When do you want me to come in?"

"The sooner you can make it here, the better."

"I'll call Trent. Once we get our things together we'll be there. I'll let you know when we're on our way."

"All right."

Nadia dressed quickly and then gathered her things, tossing them in her suitcase. She dialed Trent's number. It went to voicemail. She tried again. "Where is he?" She opened her door just as he walked by.

"Hey, you're up."

"Where were you? I was starting to get worried." She felt a deep line cross her forehead as she scrunched up her nose.

"I'm sorry; I didn't mean to worry you. I went out for a jog this morning. I needed to clear my head. Why, what's wrong?"

"I received a call from Detective Warren. He said he had some information for me, and he wants me to come in as soon as possible.

"Give me a couple minutes to get my things together and I'll be over."

Nadia pulled her suitcase behind her as she walked to the door. Looking over her shoulder, she glanced one more time around the room that had become her safe haven. She started missing it already.

She knocked on Trent's door, jumping a little when he opened it quickly. "I just wanted to let you know I'm ready. I'll be waiting out here."

"I'm almost ready. I'll be out in a couple minutes."

A nervous smile caused a twinge in her upper lip. After he shut the door, Nadia leaned back against the wall. The coolness on her back brought relief to her rattled nerves. She closed her eyes, mind replaying the events of the day before. If only she could go back there. *If only.*

The sudden breeze across her face caught her by surprise. She opened her eyes. A tall, muscular figure stood before her. Her heart skipped a beat. She wanted to run but couldn't force her feet to move. *Who is this guy? He looks familiar.*

"Sorry, ma'am, didn't mean to frighten you. I'm Officer Todd Mitchell. We spoke at the police station in Harvest Hills. I took your original statement."

"Oh, of course. I remember you now." Nadia wanted to relax, but the officer seemed agitated about something.

"I'm working with Detective Warren on your case. He said you were coming into the station today, so I'm here to escort you." He reached out his hand. "So if you'll just come with me, we can be on our way."

Nadia didn't move. Had she missed the mention of

this guy by Detective Warren? She thought over the conversation. "That's very kind of you, but I'm going to wait for Trent. We'll follow you in together."

His eyes narrowed as he stared back at her. "Miss, I'm afraid you don't understand." He grabbed her and covered her open mouth.

"If you come quietly, your friend in there won't get hurt. If you scream, well, you won't like the outcome. Is that clear?"

His rough beard scratched against her cheek as she shook her head. He removed his hand, placed it on her back and pushed her forward. "Let's go." She clamped her mouth shut against the scream. She had no choice. Trent's life depended on it. *Stay calm, Nadia. Just stay calm.*

"Good morning."

"Good morning, Ms. White." Her lips started to quiver as she smiled. The hand on her back pushed against her. "Hurry up." He whispered in an agitated voice.

Nadia lowered her head as Officer Mitchell pushed her into the front seat of a black, unmarked police car. *Lord, protect me.*

Chapter 14

Trent opened the door, "Are you ready?" He stepped into the hallway, his head turned left and right. "Nadia?"

Her door wouldn't open. His breath came faster and faster. His heart raced as he ran down the steps.

"Ms. White, have you seen Nadia this morning? Like in the last ten minutes?"

"Yes, she just walked out with a police officer, not even five minutes ago. Is everything ok?"

"No! It's not!" Trent ran outside. A man getting in a black car caught his attention. There on the passenger side sat Nadia, her face filled with fear.

"Nadia!" Their eyes met. His feet hit the concrete faster and faster. He called out her name again as they sped past him.

Trent turned and ran back up the stairs to his room, slamming the door behind him as he pulled out his phone.

"Detective Warren."

"Hello, detective, this is Trent. Some man took off with Nadia! I couldn't get to her in time!"

"Whoa, calm down. Start from the top."

Trent took a deep breath, grabbed their things from the hallway and headed for his truck. "Nadia told me this morning that you had gotten some information she needed to see. She was waiting for me in the hallway while I changed clothes and packed my suitcase. When I opened the door, I didn't see her anywhere. I tried hers but it was locked. Her suitcase was still by my door. I asked the woman at the desk if she had seen her. She said she just left with a police officer. Nadia didn't say anything about any police coming for us when I talked with her. I ran out front and saw him getting in the car. Nadia was in the passenger side. She looked scared. I called after them but he just sped by me. I'm telling you, something just isn't right here!"

"You're right Trent. Something isn't right. I gave Todd a call this morning telling him to just to follow you-all back, not bring Nadia without you."

After throwing the suitcases in the back seat of the truck, Trent climbed in and starting driving.

"So what does this mean? What do I need to do?"

"See if you can just catch up with them. If you do, call me back. I'll get some officers on it too. Now, Trent, listen to me, if you do catch up with them, just stay with them. Don't try and do anything."

Does he really expect me to do nothing when Nadia is in danger?

"Trent!"

"I'm here, detective. I won't do anything but follow them."

"I'm serious. Todd is good at what he does. That's why I put him on this case. But I don't know what he's doing or thinking right now. You have to keep yourself safe too."

Trent didn't want to admit it was the truth. "I know."

"I'll call you if I find out anything."

Slamming his phone shut, Trent tossed it on the

seat beside him. "How am I supposed to do nothing? Lord, help!"

Nadia watched Officer Mitchell out of the corner of her eye. She fought the urge to ask questions, choosing instead to pray. She looked out the window, watching as the bare landscape gave way to scattered clumps of trees.

"I'm sorry, Nadia. I had hoped that Mick -- uh -- Detective Warren -- didn't put me on this case."

"Why?"

"Nadia, you have to understand. I don't want to do this, but I have no choice." She searched his face as he looked back and forth between her and the road.

"No choice?"

"No."

"I don't believe that. We always have a choice. I'm just confused why Detective Warren would have you treat me this way."

Officer Mitchell's head faced forward as he glanced along the side of the road. Nadia grabbed the armrest as he jerked the wheel. The car came to a sudden stop, and he cut the engine.

"What are you doing?"

Minutes passed before he answered. "Nadia, Detective Warren would never order me to treat you, or anyone else, this way. My orders to take you came from someone else. He... well... he's a very dangerous man. So, you see, I had no choice. You don't know the kind of man you're up against."

Apparently he did. How? "I don't know the man

I'm up against; you're right about that. I don't have any idea who he is or what he wants with me. I'm taking it that he's the one who killed my husband and Jenny – Lily – oh, *whatever* her name was. Although why, I don't know. I don't know a lot of things right now and to tell you the truth, I'm really sick of not knowing." Her clenched fists pounded the dashboard. "You know, go ahead, take me to him. I need answers. I *want* answers."

"I can't imagine what you're going through, but when you meet him, I would advise you not to act that way."

Blood raced through her body as her heart pounded. "I've been running long enough, not even knowing who or what I am running from. I think this mysterious man should answer my questions."

Wow, where did that boldness come from?

"You do deserve answers, Nadia; I'm just not sure you'll want them."

She closed her eyes. "You know what all this is about, don't you?"

The engine roared to life again. "Yes, unfortunately I do," he said as he pulled back onto the road.

"I guess you're not going to tell me?"

"That wouldn't be very wise on my part."

"What about his name? Can you at least tell me that?"

"His name is Nick… Nick Comings."

Silence filled the air between them. Her thoughts ran wild. *Who's Nick Comings?* His last name was the same as Eric's; as hers when they were married, but what did this mean?

Nadia rolled down the window, inhaling the smells of the last flowers of the season. Her eyes squinted at the bright sun. The humming rhythm of the tires against the blacktop helped slow her pounding heart.

"How do you know him? How do you know Nick?"

Officer Mitchell squirmed. *He should've known I was going to ask.*

"I had a run in with him a couple months back. He's wanted for several things; not only here. An anonymous call came in about a robbery in progress. I was the first one at the scene. Nick took off running out the back door when I entered the house. I chased after him. He was just a couple steps in front me when, out of nowhere, I felt something clamp down on my leg. I fell down face first. Two big dogs were on top of me before I could roll over."

He wiped the beaded sweat from his forehead. "A gunshot rang out; then another. The dogs were dead. Nick squatted down next to me and held my chin up with the barrel of his gun. He said, *"You owe me one."* He took off when he heard the other officers coming. They took me to the hospital. I needed stitches on my legs, arms and neck. Those dogs didn't have me down long, but they did a number on me." He shook his head. "I wish I had caught him then. I wouldn't be in this mess right now."

Nadia's voice shook. "I guess I'm what you 'owe' him?"

"Yes."

Chapter 15

Nadia stretched out her legs as much as possible in the cramped space in front of her. Closing her eyes, she brought the memory of the sheltered place in the woods to mind again. Such peace filled "their place". A slight smile raised one corner of her lips.

"Why are you smiling? This isn't a situation to be smiling over."

"Officer Mitchell, I have come to realize I'm not in control of anything this life throws at me. If I prefer my last memories on this earth to be good ones, and smile about them, why does that bother you?"

He didn't respond.

"I don't know what the next few hours hold for me, but I do know the one who will be holding me through them. I find my rest and peace in him. I was blessed enough to have met a wonderful man, who I know is doing everything he can to get to me right now, and I'm thanking the Lord for the moments we shared not long before you took me. That is where my peace and smile come from. They are God-given."

Officer Mitchell shook his head. "How can you even believe in a god, let along *the* God, with all that's happened to you? Where is he? Why isn't he saving you from all this? You're innocent!" His hardened fist hit the steering wheel, causing him to swerve.

"Officer Mitchell, my God is here with me. His peace surrounds me. I trust him to do what's best for my life."

"What's best for your life!" he scoffed. "Even if that means your death?"

"We all will die one way or another, Officer Mitchell. I choose to believe God will be the judge of when and where, not myself."

Chapter 16

Trent let off the gas as the black unmarked police cruiser turned down a long gravel driveway. *Great, how do I stay unnoticed now?*

He pulled onto the gravel road and stopped. As he dialed Detective Warren's number, the car increased the distance between them but stayed in sight.

"What do I do now?" he asked after filling Detective Warren in on the location.

"Sit tight. I know where you're at; I'm just a few minutes behind you. I have backup coming too."

"I don't know where this drive leads. What if I lose them?"

"You won't lose them. That drive leads to an old farmhouse back there. Just sit tight and wait for me, Trent. I'm only a couple minutes away."

Sit tight and wait! How am I supposed to do that? Trent wanted to press the gas pedal down until it hit the floor. He didn't care anymore who saw him; he only wanted to get to Nadia. "I'm not doing a very good job of keeping her safe, God!"

Peace filled the cab of his truck as a gentle voice spoke to his spirit. *"That's my job. Wait for the others."*

How could he argue with God?

"Yes, Lord. I'm not liking this, but I trust you."

He drummed on the steering wheel as he waited. "This is one of the hardest things I've ever had to do."

His head thumped lightly on the headrest as he closed his eyes. The crunch of tires approaching filled his ears but he kept his mind focused on his prayer. When he looked up he saw Detective Warren pull in front of his truck, followed by three more police cruisers. His phone rang.

"Hello?"

"Trent, I know you don't want to hear this. However, for everyone's safety, I need you to stay where you are. Do not follow us."

"What? Are you serious? I waited here for you! I knew I should've followed them," he said through gritted teeth, trying to keep his frustration in check.

"I'll call you."

He listened to silence on the other end of the line for only a second before tossing his phone in the empty seat beside him.

He shut the truck door behind him, got on his knees and began to wage war against the enemy no one could see.

Chapter 17

Officer Mitchell opened the door and waited for Nadia to get out.

"I guess we're here?"

"Not yet, we have to walk the rest of the way. There's a barn just over that hill. Nick's waiting for us there."

"Well, let's get this show on the road, then." She pushed back the tall grass and forced her feet to move through it. He held onto her arm as he walked beside her.

The old barn door creaked as Officer Mitchell pulled it open. Small pieces of wood fell to the ground. Tiny dust particles floated in the stream of light that filled the emptiness in front of her. Her hand covered her mouth as she heaved. The smell of rotting hay and decaying animals filled her nostrils.

"After you, Nadia."

There was only one explanation about why she wasn't consumed with fear right now. Any normal person would be. *So this is what the peace that passes all understanding feels like.*

Slowly she stepped inside and waited for Officer Mitchell, but the only thing she heard was the creak of the door as it shut behind her leaving her in an unknown darkness. She stood motionless, waiting for her eyes to adjust. A silhouette emerged a few inches in front of her.

"Well, well, well. How nice of you to join me, *Nadia.* I've been waiting a long time to meet you." His warm breath blew against her, and her skin prickled at the sound of her name.

"What do you want with me?"

"That's a long story; one that has changed along the way."

"Changed?"

"Yes, but I'll fill you in after I introduce myself." Suddenly the lights in the barn kicked on one by one along the ceiling. Nadia squinted. She still couldn't make out the face of the man in front her. Not until the last light kicked on right over them.

"Oh!" Her shaking hand covered her mouth. Stepping back, she stumbled over the pile of hay behind her and fell.

"Scare you, did I?" An evil grin appeared on his face; that face she thought she had known and loved.

"You look just like...Eric. My mind wasn't playing tricks on me."

"No, it wasn't, although I have to admit, it was kind of fun watching you squirm."

"That's not right." She struggled to get her feet underneath her. "You shouldn't play with people's minds and emotions like that."

"You're right, it isn't. But I never said I was trying to do the right thing, did I? You might want to stay seated for what's coming next."

"I prefer to stand."

"Okay, suit yourself. My name is Nick; I'm Eric's twin brother. I'll spare you the boring childhood details, and get to the good parts. Eric and I were close when we were kids. Through our teenage years we grew apart, until finally one day we got in a disagreement that led to a fistfight, and, well, long story short, I got kicked out. I lost touch with everyone after awhile. A few years passed, and I ran into Eric again. I needed some ..." a sinister grin crossed his face, "I guess you could say, *help,* with some things. Eric, being the sweet, gullible person he was, wanted to mend our past and start over. He was so eager. It was kind of sad and pathetic, really. But, that's what I expected of him. What I didn't expect was him getting cold feet and leaving me on this - oh, what shall we call it in the presence of a lady? - Let's go with 'adventure'. Almost cost me my freedom that night. Thankfully, I got away. Thanks to the help of some dogs. And Lily. She got out with what we came for. Rest her soul. I'm going to miss her. Eric and I had known her since we were little."

Nick stopped pacing. He stood in front of her, staring. She gritted her teeth as he placed his hot hand on her arm. A cold emptiness in his eyes.

"Needless to say, I wasn't very happy with my brother's betrayal. I kept my eye on him and waited for the right time. Little did I know it would only be a couple of weeks later. But hey, when the door opens, you walk through it, right?"

Nadia didn't answer.

"I thought you might not agree with me."

"Why didn't Eric tell me about you?"

"Why do men keep secrets from their wives? I can't answer that one. I'm not married...*yet.*"

"What do you mean?"

"What do I mean? Well, your taking off kind of makes it easy to start our lives fresh as Eric and Nadia Comings."

"But Eric's dead. This will never work."

"Sure it will. New town, new life. All I need is

Eric's death certificate."

"I don't have it."

She gulped at the tightened grip of his hand on her chin. "What do you mean you don't have it?"

"It was in my house. It got burned up."

The slap snapped her head sideways. A single tear cooled the heat a little.

"You kept papers like that in your house, you stupid woman?"

The creak of the door cut off his rant. "What do you want, Todd? It better be good!"

"Sorry, Nick; the cops are here. They just went into the house. It won't be long until they make their way over here."

"Someone is always messing up my plans!" The rage in his voice caused her to jump.

"Get her out of here. Hide in the tall brush out there until they get in here. I'll stall them, and then we'll get her to my house."

"Yes, sir." Officer Mitchell's hand wrapped around Nadia's and he pulled her toward the tall brush outside the barn.

"There they go!" She heard someone yell. She would've screamed had it not been for the gun pressed against her side.

"It's clear. Let's go." Officer Mitchell pulled her up the hill and forced her back into the car.

Detective Warren stepped out onto the porch just as they turned the car around. She glanced at her captor. He didn't seem to have noticed. Knowing Detective Warren had seen her helped her to remain hopeful. *Thank you, God.*

Chapter 18

Trent had just got back in his truck and shut the door when his phone rang. "Hello?"

"They're headed your way, Trent. Stay with them. I'll be right behind you!"

Reaching down, he turned the key and waited. *Hopefully he'll stop when he sees my truck.*

Trent saw the dust cloud from the approaching black car. Officer Mitchell was not slowing down.

Trent didn't move.

The black cruiser flew past him and onto the highway. Trent turned and followed, watching as Officer Mitchell weaved in and out of traffic.

Trent's heart pounded as the crash unfolded before him, *"NO! Lord, please!"* Gravel flew up around Trent's truck. Finally making it to where the overturned car had landed, he slammed on the brakes.

The truck door flung open. He ran to the passenger side. His adrenaline-fueled fist hammered the window. "Nadia, wake up! Nadia! Do you hear me? Wake up! *Nadia!*"

He pulled the phone from his pocket.

"911, what's your emergency?"

"There's been an accident. We're on Highway 22 Southbound about thirty minutes past the Harvest Hills exit. A car overturned in the ditch and there are injuries. Please hurry; I can't get her out!"

"Sir, please take a moment to calm down, and then

tell me as much of what you can see as possible."

Trent breathed. "The lady in the passenger side is bleeding from her head pretty badly. She's unconscious. I haven't seen any movement from her since I've been here."

For the first time his eyes looked beyond where Nadia was. "The driver looks to be unconscious as well."

"Very good, sir, all that was relayed directly to the ambulance, and they will be there within ten minutes. Hang in there: they are coming as fast as they can."

"Thank you."

A reflection in the window caught Trent's attention and he jumped up. Detective Warren stepped back.

"I'm sorry, I didn't hear you pull up. I can't get her to respond."

"I'm sure she'll be fine." Detective Warren placed his hand on Trent's shoulder.

Sirens closing in turned their attention back to the scene before them.

"It feels like I'm in some kind of movie, with everything in slow motion."

"Help is here, Trent. Let's let them do their jobs. She'll be ok."

"You can't promise me what only God is able to give ..." His voice cracked. "... and take away."

He watched as they dragged Nadia's limp body from the car and placed her on the stretcher. Walking beside her, he grabbed her hand. "Please wait just a moment," he said before they lifted her up into the back of the ambulance. "Nadia I'm here. I love you, and I'll meet you at the hospital. Squeeze my hand if you can hear me, please." He willed the slightest squeeze to come, but it didn't.

His hand fell from hers as the stretcher lifted up and locked into place. The doors shut.

He turned, expecting to see his truck, but it was blocked from his view.

"Are you sure you are okay to drive?"

"Yes."

"I'd best see what's going on with Officer Mitchell. I'll catch up with you at the hospital."

He watched as the detective carefully made his way over to the car. Another stretcher popped up into view, covered with a sheet.

"Sorry, Detective; Officer Mitchell didn't make it."

Detective Warren stopped in his tracks. His shoulders slumped. Trent shook his head and continued to his truck. *All this tragedy, and for what?* He pulled away.

Chapter 19

Nadia's eyes opened to a blinding bright light as she groggily took in the white walls. The strong smell of disinfectant reached her nose. Sitting up, her hand quickly flew to her throbbing head. A moan escaped her trembling lips as tears began to run down her cheeks. She opened her mouth to call out just as Trent walked through the door.

"Nadia, you're awake. I'll get the nurse. Lie back down!"

Is it that bad?

A woman walked through the door, followed by Trent.

"Hello, Ms. Lucas, my name's Maggie. I'm your nurse today." She looked Nadia over as she gently checked her pulse. "How are you feeling?"

"My head really hurts."

Maggie pulled a folded up piece of paper and a pen from her pocket and wrote down her notes. "I bet it does. That was some cut you got up there. It's pretty swollen. It will take a few days for it to go down."

Maggie faced Trent. "The doctor usually stops by around noon. Will you be able to stay until then?"

"Yes. I will be here."

The nurse glanced at the clock that hung above Nadia's bed. "It's time for your pain medicine. I'll be back with it in a couple of minutes. Would you like some water to drink?"

"Yes please." *Hopefully, that will take the cottony feeling away.*

Trent sat down in the chair beside her. His strong, steady hand felt good wrapped around hers. He lifted his head; tears filled his eyes. "Squeeze my hand, Nadia."

Delicate, fragile fingers began to bend around his, accompanied by a weak squeeze.

The corners of his mouth rose as a faint sigh escaped from his lips.

"What happened, Trent?"

His smile faded as he closed his eyes. "I'll tell you after the nurse comes back in. That way I won't be interrupted."

Numbness coursed through her at the pain on Trent's face. *I guess it was that bad.*

The door clicked. The nurse smiled at Nadia. "Here's your water and pain medication." She handed Nadia a glass and a little white cup that held two pills. "I'll be back to check on you in about an hour or so. In the meantime, if you need anything…" she placed the call button and remote next to Nadia's leg, "…just press this button for the nurses' station. It's right outside your door. This one is for the TV."

"Thank you."

"Don't overdo it. Remember your body still needs its rest," she called before shutting the door behind her.

Nadia took her medicine and then turned towards Trent. "She's gone. Please tell me."

Trent took several deep breaths. "After Officer Mitchell took you this morning, I called Detective

Warren. He told me to follow you. I caught up with you-all about twenty minutes past the Harvest Hills exit. He instructed me to wait while he tried to go in and get you. I wanted so badly to follow him down that drive, but I didn't. I stayed there and prayed."

"I could feel you praying for me - " Her body grew tense as her hands grabbed the blanket that lay over her.

"Nadia, what's wrong?"

"Officer Mitchell took me to meet Nick."

"Who's Nick?"

"Eric's twin brother."

"What?"

"I'm sorry, Trent. I didn't mean to interrupt. The gravel drive made me remember about Nick."

Trent held her hand. "It's all right. Go on."

"He wanted to take over Eric's life. He wanted me to pretend that he was Eric. How does someone even think of those things? I wondered if that was what Detective Warren wanted to tell me."

"Wow. I don't even know what to say to that." His head shook. "He'll be here in a little while. We'll find out then."

A loud rumble filled the silence. "Wow, that's embarrassing."

Nadia's laughter quickly brought her hand to her head, "Ouch! Don't make me laugh; that hurts."

"Sorry. I'll do my best to keep my empty stomach quiet."

"Go get you something to eat, Trent. I'll be fine. I'm going to lie here and close my eyes."

"I'm not leaving you."

"I'm fine. Go get something to eat."

She smiled as he drummed his fingers against the bed. "Stop thinking about it and go already. The nurse's desk is right out there. I'll be fine."

"Okay, but I'll be back in just a few minutes."

"Okay."

Chapter 20

Deep in an all-too-real dream, piercing blue eyes filled with hate and anger glared at her, joined by an evil grin and low, growling laughter.

Nadia's eyes darted frantically back and forth under damp, closed eyelids. Sweat bubbled up around her hairline. Her pulse raced. That stare, it bored right through her; *so real.*

Her eyes popped open. Looking around the room as she tried to slow her breathing down, the slight sound of a click drew her attention to the door. Not a muscle in her body wanted to move, but she forced her hand to slide down beside her leg to where the remote and call button had been placed earlier.

Nothing.

She checked the place where the nurse had gotten them from. There they hung.

She raised her hand and stretched up as far as she could. It was no use. They were out of reach. *Great!*

"How are we feeling after a short nap; any better?" The nurse asked as she walked in the door.

Nadia didn't want the alarm to come through in her voice. She answered as nonchalantly as possible. "Yes, I'm feeling a bit better, thanks."

"That's great. Sorry I'm a little late in checking in on you. I didn't want to disturb your meeting with the detective."

"The detective?" Nadia's nose scrunched.

"Did it go that badly?" Maggie shook her head. "I knew I should've had him come back and talk to you when you were awake. I'm sorry. I won't let it happen again."

"No, Maggie, you don't understand. I just woke up, right before you came in. The detective wasn't here."

"Sure he was. He showed me a badge and everything. Of course it was hard to get past those blue eyes. I think they'd draw any woman in." Her smile seemed like it could touch her ears, but the corners of her mouth dropped back to their normal place at the look on Nadia's face.

"How long was he in here?"

"About thirty minutes."

"Maggie, I need you to listen to me. That was not, I repeat *not* a police detective. That man's name is Nick Comings. He's after me."

"Oh!"

"Will you please hand me the phone, remote, and call button again?"

Maggie looked up at the things that were back in their original places. She handed the phone and remote back to Nadia, but held onto the call button. "I'll give this to you in a minute." Maggie pushed the button.

The door swung open as two nurses ran in. "What's going on?"

"I need both of you to stay in here with her for a few minutes while I'll call the head of security." Maggie pointed at them. "Whatever you do, do not leave her. I want you to check around the room and make sure nothing was tampered with." She patted Nadia's hand, "I'll be back in a few minutes."

The nurses hurriedly went about the task while Nadia called Trent.

He answered on the third ring. "Hello?"

Tears rolled faster down her cheeks as she tried to talk through the sobs. "Trent, he was here! Nick was in my room!"

"What? When?"

"He just now left."

"I'll be right up. I'm down in the cafeteria."

"I have nurses with me right now. Please just find him."

"Were you awake when he was there?"

"No, I woke up as he was leaving. I heard the door click shut. I thought maybe it was the nurse, but when I reached for the call button and couldn't find it, I remembered something that seemed like a dream ... his face ... his eyes ..."

"I should have never left you."

"Don't say that. You need to take care of yourself, too."

"No, I need to take care of you, and I've failed at that twice now."

"Trent, stop talking like that. This is not your fault. None of it is. I brought you into all this, remember?"

Silence.

"I'm going to call Detective Warren and see where he's at."

"Okay."

She flipped her phone shut and watched the nurses check over everything as she waited for him to call back.

Minutes passed before Maggie walked back into

the room. "Nadia, there is a guard at your door now, and we have a sketch artist making a picture of Nick to hang up out there, with a number to call if anyone sees him." Maggie turned toward the other nurses. "Is everything the way it should be in here?"

"Everything seems to be fine," they answered in unison.

"You may go." She faced Nadia. "Are you okay?"

"I think so."

"Your call buttons are there beside you. Don't hesitate to call if you need me."

"I won't, trust me."

Nadia waited until Maggie closed the door before she breathed out heavily and whispered a prayer.

A tall, stout man stepped into her room.

"Miss, my name is Garrett. I'm the guard stationed outside your door. A Detective Warren and a Trent Macalister are here to see you; is that okay?"

"Yes, please let them in."

The guard stepped out of the way, motioned for them to enter the room, and closed the door behind them.

Detective Warren stood off to the side, silently waiting as Trent held Nadia in his arms. Finally he cleared his throat.

Trent released Nadia and sat down next to the bed. Her hand wrapped in his.

Detective Warren sat down and opened a note pad. Nadia told what she remembered. "I'll be sure to talk with Maggie before I leave." He looked down at his watch. "I guess I better go talk to her now, if I can. When I get back, if you're up to it, I'll fill you in on what I found out before all this happened." He stood up and laid the pad down in the chair and walked out.

Nadia turned to Trent. "Any news on Nick?"

"There's an officer by each exit and some on patrol around the hospital, and searching the surrounding blocks. They're hoping he didn't make it very far."

"I hope they catch him."

"They will, Nadia."

His smile helped to calm her nerves.

"Do you mind if I turn on the television?"

"Of course not; why would I?"

"I just wanted to be polite and ask first."

She picked up the remote and handed it to him. The room filled with the voices of the evening news reporters. A picture came up on the screen, a rough artist's sketch of Nick's face. "This is breaking news. Please contact the police if you see this man. He is believed to be very dangerous; murder and kidnapping are just two of the things he is wanted in questioning for. His name is Nick Comings. Again, please call the police if you see him. In other news ..."

Nadia's eyes stayed glued to the television even after his picture was gone. She saw Trent watching her out of the corner of her eye.

"Sounds like the detective is back," Trent said as he tilted his head towards the door. "I'll shut this off for now."

Detective Warren walked in, followed by Maggie.

"I came in to check on you one more time before I head home." The cool metal of the stethoscope touched her skin. "Heart sounds good. Can you lean forward a little bit for me so I can listen to your lungs? Great; everything sounds good." After writing a few things down on the folded piece of paper, she patted Nadia's hand and nodded her head toward Trent and Detective Warren. "I'll see you tomorrow."

Detective Warren waited until the door closed before asking if they wanted to hear the news tonight or wait until tomorrow. After a short silence, Nadia whispered, "Tonight."

A thick folder sat on Detective Warren's lap.

Nadia's heart pounded as he opened it. Trent's strong hand wrapped a little more firmly around hers.

"I guess I'll start at the beginning." Detective Warren cleared his throat. "I was finally able to get a hold of Chester and Molly Comings. I talked with them for awhile, finding out a lot of information about Nick especially. Molly told me that the boys were close and had a happy childhood. You could hardly separate them. However, everything changed after they got into high school. Nick started hanging out with the wrong crowd. He started drinking, which led down the path to drugs, stealing, and fighting. They tried to talk with Nick; tried to get him help, but it didn't work. In fact, he just got worse. He ended up starting stuff by pretending to be Eric; stealing his girlfriends, getting him in trouble at school. The list went on and on.

Finally, Eric got tired of it and stood up for himself. That resulted in a big fight and both boys ending up in the ER. That was the last straw for Molly. After much discussion, she and Chester decided to tell Nick that he had to move out. The boys were in their senior year then and over eighteen. They haven't spoken with Nick since that day. Eric stayed around for awhile. He didn't want to leave his parents in case Nick came back. A year later, he moved here to attend college. Everything seemed to be going well until one day Molly got a call from Eric saying that some of the people he went to college with actually knew Nick. She said the thought of possibly seeing his brother again, after almost four years, made him happy. She knew Eric missed Nick. Even after everything that happened, he still loved his brother.

Molly had her doubts, though, and told him to be careful. After that, calls from Eric came less and less often. She wondered if what she had said had driven a wedge between them. She tried calling him at least twice a week, but was lucky to talk to him once a month. She noticed a change in him. His voice wasn't as alive and filled with joy the way it once was. He always sounded tired. He told her it was from working and classes, but she said she didn't believe him. She didn't know about you, your marriage, or his death."

"He did seem down or something when I met him," Nadia said. "He told me that I had saved his life; that I had given him a reason to live again. I thought he was just being romantic. I guess you never really know somebody, do you?"

Trent's hand rubbed up and down her arm. She longed to feel his comforting touch, but she couldn't. Her body was numb. "So, I guess Lily, Jenny ... " Her hands flew up. " ... Whatever her name was...I guess she *was* in on the whole thing. He told me today that he planned on taking over Eric's life, and wanted the death certificate. He wasn't happy when I told him it burned in the fire. He wanted me to pretend he was

Eric, and that Nick was the one who died. How can people be that cruel?"

"I'm not sure, Ms. Lucas." Detective Warren rubbed his chin. "This is what I'm thinking. Nick and Lily were going to take over Eric's life and yours, but when Lily burned down your house, it caused a shift in his plans. Nick decided to get rid of her for her betrayal, and be with you."

"So." It was hard to form their names on her lips. "Nick and Lily were going to take over *our* lives." She gripped the sheets tightly, her knuckles white, as moisture met her cheeks more rapidly with each blink. "They meant to kill us both."

Detective Warren slowly nodded his head. "Yes, unfortunately, we believe that was his initial plan."

"Why?"

"That we don't know. To be honest, I'm not sure if we ever will. This is what I've come up with. You weren't there the day Nick came to the house and killed Eric. After finding out you had moved they followed you, and Lily got a job working for you, to keep track of you, mostly, it seems. Maybe they intended to finish out their plan this weekend. But Trent showed up."

"*If I was you I'd take off and have a nice relaxing weekend.*" The words made her entire body shake. How close they had come to pulling it all off.

"I'm not feeling too good right now. My head hurts for more reasons than the accident. I'm going to try and get some sleep. In the morning maybe all this will make more sense to me."

"I'll see myself out." Detective Warren turned toward Trent. "If you have any questions please let me know."

"We will, thanks."

Worn out physically, mentally, and emotionally, Nadia let sleep overtake her.

Chapter 21

"Breakfast time!" a sweet-sounding voice called out, rousing Nadia from a perfect night's sleep. Rubbing her eyes, she opened them and focused on a woman about her age laying a plate of food on the tray.

"Do you need help sitting up before I move this over in front of you?"

Nadia smiled. "No." She scooted herself back a little. "But thank you."

"I can't promise this will taste good, but it sure does smell good."

"I agree. It smells wonderful."

Nadia lifted the cover off the plate. Her mouth watered at the pancakes and sausages. A small bowl of strawberries sat off to the side next to a container of juice.

"I'll be back around in an hour. Enjoy your breakfast."

"Thanks."

She savored the taste, eating every bite as slowly as her stomach would allow. She had been finished for about ten minutes when the nurse and doctor came in. After checking her over, the doctor removed her bandages and checked the wound. "It's healing nicely. I won't be able to take the stitches out until next week though. But I see no reason, if you're ready that is, for you not to be able to go home today."

Excitement engulfed her.

"I'm taking it the joker-like smile means you're ready?"

Nadia laughed out loud. "Yes doctor, I'm ready."

"Wonderful. I'll get the paperwork all together and hopefully have you out of here by noon. Sound good?"

"Sounds great!"

For the first time since all this happened, the fact that she no longer had a home to go to surfaced from its pleasant hiding place. The excitement died out of her eyes.

"Why the sad look?"

"I just remembered I don't have a home to go to."

"We'll get all that taken care of. For now, how would you like to go back to my uncle's hotel? We still have our rooms."

"We do?"

"Well, we never officially checked out," he smiled.

"No, I guess we didn't."

"So, how does that sound to you? Or if you want some place closer, we can do that."

The idea of going back to the hotel caused a small grin to form. But she knew there was a job to get back to for both of them. "As wonderful as that sounds, I think I'll get a place around here. I do need to get back to work, and so do you. That would be a long drive."

"I suppose you're right."

"Speaking of which, we need to call Mr. Caldwell. Can you hand me the phone?"

He sat it down beside her. "I know a hotel close to

my apartment. I'll go ahead and check it out and get you a room while we're waiting for your release forms. That way it will be ready to go when you get there."

"Thank you, Trent. I appreciate that. If you hand me my purse, I'll get you some cash."

"I don't think so." He called over his shoulder as he closed the door behind him.

"Oh, that man. What am I going do with him?"

Nadia talked to Mr. Caldwell while she waited for Trent to return. He had agreed to let them both use a vacation day and return to work on Tuesday. She grabbed a pen and piece of paper and started a list of other people she needed to call. "Let's see, there's Mr. Caldwell." She checked his name off. "Next is the insurance companies and Mindy."

House hunting again was not what she wanted to be doing this weekend, but neither was living too long in a hotel room.

An hour passed before she heard the familiar click of the door. "Hotel is all taken care of."

"Thank you."

"You're welcome, Nadia."

The way her name rolled off his tongue sent shivers through her body. *I'm not ready for another relationship, Lord. Am I?*

Trent took her hand in his and cleared his throat. Nadia jumped. "Sorry, I didn't mean to scare you."

She could feel the warmth fill her cheeks. "You didn't."

His raised eyebrow made her laugh.

"I didn't, huh?"

"Okay, maybe a little. Oh, I talked with Mr. Caldwell. He said we can use a vacation day today and return to work tomorrow. I've also made a list of the people I need to call as soon as we get to the hotel."

"You sound on top of things."

"I just want to get it all out of the way."

"I can understand that."

"Can I ask another favor of you?"

"Sure."

"I didn't pack any work clothes. Do you think we could stop somewhere so I can get a couple new outfits?"

"Not a problem."

"Great, thanks. I wish they would hurry up. I am so ready to get out of here. So," she squeezed his hand. "Have you talked any more with Detective Warren?"

"No. I was planning to call him when we got you settled in the hotel room. I can call him now if you prefer."

"No, after I get settled in is fine with me."

Nadia sat quietly as the nurse checked over her stats one more time before removing all the hookups.

"Everything looks good. Here's your paperwork and your prescription. After you read these over, just sign at the bottom; then you'll be free to go. Just leave the gown on the bed on your way out."

Nadia read over the papers and signed her name. The sooner she was out of there the better.

"Trent, would you help me get up? My legs feel kind of weak."

She sat up, flopped her legs over the side of the bed, and grabbed Trent's outstretched hands. Her bare feet rested on the cool floor.

Trent led her to the open bathroom door. She held onto the sink as he grabbed her clothes from the closet. She dressed as quickly as her wobbly legs and weak arms would allow and then stepped out.

"I think I found my legs again."

"That's good."

He looked her up and down; his face showed that he disagreed. "You sit down for a minute, I'll be right back." She started to protest, but thought better of it and sat down on the edge of the bed with a smile on her face.

"I could have made it," she sighed. *But I'm glad he cares enough not to let me try.*

"Here's your chariot, madam."

"Oh, and what a lovely chariot it is!"

Trent pushed the wheelchair that had a dark green flag on a pole over to where Nadia sat. Taking her hand he helped her down into the chair. "Are you comfortable?"

"Yes, sir."

"Away we go."

The guard held the door open as Trent pushed the chair through, and then followed them, and an aid who took over wheelchair duties, to the front doors.

"Thank you."

"You're welcome, ma'am."

Trent walked around the car and got in. "What store would you like to go to?"

"The cheapest one."

Two hours and five new outfits later, they pulled into a parking lot in front of the hotel. "Let's get you settled in, and then we'll make those phone calls and get something to eat."

Chapter 22

Nadia grabbed the remote control off the bedside table and flipped on the television as she waited for Trent to return with the food. It felt good to put her feet up and rest after the long shopping trip.

She pulled the crumpled list of people and places to call out of her purse and flattened it out as much as she could.

She ended the call with Mindy after Trent came through the door. She breathed in the smell of the warm sub and fries sitting in front of her. "This smells so good, I can't wait to dig in."

Her hand met Trent's and their heads bowed as he blessed the food. "Now you may 'dig in' as you put it." His wink caused a shiver down her spine. *How does he do that?*

"Who were you talking to?"

Nadia chewed and savored the taste in her mouth before answering. His comical stare made her grin.

"Good, is it?"

"Yes it is; and I was talking with my friend Mindy. I asked her to keep a look out for a house. She is in real estate."

"Oh, yes, I remember now."

"She's the one that helped me find the house I lived in before."

"What areas are you looking in?" Trent asked between bites.

"Anywhere close to work, I guess. I don't want to drive real far in the winter months."

"Driving in the snow isn't all bad."

"Maybe not for you in that big ol' truck of yours, but my car…" The realization of not having a car hit her. "I need a car."

"We'll get that taken care of. You called the insurance company, right?"

"Yes. But who knows how long that's going to take? They don't get in a hurry, you know."

"I'll make some phone calls and see what I can do."

"You've done enough all ready. I'll figure out something. Anyway, Mindy's going to look around and see what she can find. Hopefully set something up for this weekend. I was wondering if you would like to come with us."

"I would love to. Just let me know when."

Nadia rubbed her head. "I don't mean to be rude, but I'd really like to lie down and get some sleep."

"You're not being rude. I'll call you in the morning." He looked back when she didn't answer. "Nadia, what's wrong?"

"I've tried to ignore this feeling of guilt. It's just not working."

"You have nothing to feel guilty about."

"Yes, I do."

"How many times do I have to tell you that you are more important to me than anything else, next to God of course. Nadia, I don't think you know how much I care for you."

She felt the warmth in her cheeks. She could only guess at how red they were. "I guess I'm afraid you're going to wake up one day and realize how crazy this all is and leave. Which I couldn't and wouldn't blame you for. I mean, Nick is still out there. Who knows where, or what he'll do." *There.* Her fear was finally out.

Trent's silence caused her to look up as a tear rolled down her cheek. "Well, I guess you leave me no other option than to prove to you that I'm here to stay."

She watched as he stood up, pulled something out of his pants pocket, and knelt in front of her. Her stomach flip-flopped as she focused her eyes on the little black box.

Trent gently lifted her head and their eyes met. "Nadia, my world began the moment I saw you. I was drawn to you for reasons only God knew. I feel complete when I am with you and lost when I am not. I have loved you for awhile now. We were thrown together by strange events no doubt, but the Lord knows what he's doing. I have prayed for a sweet, kind, humble, and loving woman, and she's sitting here looking at me right now. I have never been more sure of anything in my life. Nadia, will you marry me?"

So many emotions ran through her as she sat staring into Trent's eyes. Her hand shook slightly in his. Tears streamed down her face. Her smile widened. "Yes, Trent, I will marry you."

He stretched up and pressed a gentle, passionate kiss to her lips as he slid the ring on her finger. Taking her face in his hands, he looked her in the eyes. "Nadia, you have made me the happiest man on earth. Cheesy saying, I know, but it's true."

"And you have made me the happiest woman on earth. Cheesy saying, I know, but it is true."

Laughter filled the room as he wrapped her in his arms. "I love you, Nadia."

"I love you too, Trent."

Minutes passed as she enjoyed the warmth and safety in his arms. She pulled away and looked down at the diamond on her finger. "It's so beautiful."

"Nowhere near as beautiful as you are."

Chapter 23

"Would you like to talk about wedding plans?" His voice startled her.

Trent laughed. "Did I scare you?"

Rolled eyes answered his question.

"I'm sorry, I didn't mean to."

She shook her head, fighting back the laugh that wanted to escape. "I would love to talk about our wedding!"

"Good." His lips pressed against her forehead. "What should we talk about first?"

A slight smile formed on Nadia's lips. *He's going to be sorry he asked that question.*

"I don't know. There's so much to do. The invitations, the cake, the food, my dress…" She looked up, caught the fear in his eyes, and fought back a really big laugh. "…the favors, drinks…"

"Okay, okay." He wiped the sweat from his forehead. "I get it there's a lot to do. More than I realized, I have to admit…but can we please do one thing at a time?"

Nadia was no longer able to hold her laugh back. "Sure, one thing at a time it is. What would you like to start with?"

He met her raised eyebrow and smile with one of his own. "How about the most important one?"

"Which is?"

"The date."

"Oh. I guess that would be important, wouldn't it?"

"Call me crazy, but yes, I would think so."

"Do you have a certain time in mind?"

"I do."

"Care to share?"

"I was thinking sometime in the spring."

"I like that." She said. "New beginnings."

"That's exactly what I was thinking."

"What about sometime in early May?"

"Early May sounds perfect."

Chapter 24

"I've found the right house for you!" Nadia held the phone away from her ear. A slight chuckle escaped her. "Wow, Mindy, you seem a little excited about this one."

"Oh, Nadia, I am. It's perfect for you and Trent. I just know it. Get a pen and piece of paper and I will give you the address. I've already called the listing agent. We can go see it in an hour."

"An *hour?*"

"I know, Nadia, but I'm telling you, this one you are going to love. I would not have set it up if I didn't believe it was the one for you both!"

"All right, Mindy; I trust you. We'll see you in an hour." She scribbled the address on the napkin next to her plate; containing a laugh at Trent's scrunched up face. "She said it's *perfect* for us."

He took a big drink of Coke. "That's what she said about the last three we looked at."

"I know, I know, but maybe this one really is. We won't know if we don't check it out."

"I suppose you're right."

An hour later Trent pulled his truck into the long, blacktopped driveway lined with red maples. At the end they saw a light-colored brick ranch. A wooden porch stretched the length of the front. A flowerbed sat off to the left of the front door, filled with pink and purple geraniums. A walkway connected the porch to the circular driveway. On the right was a two-car garage with a breezeway connecting it to the house.

Nadia's jaw dropped. "*Wow!*"

Mindy opened the door and stepped out onto the porch, waving her hand for them to hurry and come inside.

Nadia shook her head and closed her mouth.

"So, what do you think?" The excitement in Mindy's voice sent a fresh wave of happiness coursing through Nadia.

"It's…. it's lovely, Mindy."

"Wait until you see the inside."

Reaching out, Nadia took Trent's hand and followed Mindy through the front door. Mindy stood waiting with a smile on her face.

"It's that good, huh?"

"I believe it is!"

Trent stepped aside, letting Nadia walk through the door first. Her eyes quickly scanned the room in front of her. "I'm already picturing where I can put things!"

Trent put his arm around her. "All new things: new house, new clothes, new furniture, new car, new everything; to go with our new life." He tilted her head up. "It's a fresh, new start for both of us." How could she *not* smile at that?

"You're right Trent. A fresh new start for both of us." The words felt strange, but brought back the fading smile she had just a moment ago.

"Ok, Mindy, take us on the grand tour."

"Off to your left is the living room. As you can see, there's a door off the back wall; it leads to a bedroom that has its own bath as well." Mindy motioned for them to follow. "It would be a good guest bedroom."

They walked through the open door past Mindy. Nadia stood in the middle of the room and looked around. "It would; it's a good size."

Mindy gestured to the door. "Are you ready to see more?"

"Yes, please. Lead the way."

They followed her through the archway that joined the living room and the kitchen. "Back here is the family room, dining room, and kitchen. All open, Nadia, just they way you like it. The counters are dark marble and the appliances are stainless steel. The bay window looks out over a huge fenced in yard."

Nadia stood in front of the window and imagined a yard full of toys and children. Her eyes lost focus, looking into the future.

"Earth to Nadia," Mindy giggled.

Turning around, Nadia met two faces full of questions. "*What?* I was just thinking. Let's move on."

"Already seeing children out there playing, huh? While you and Trent get dinner ready, I bet."

Heat filled her cheeks. "No!" *I really am too transparent.*

Trent's crooked grin made her breath catch in her throat.

"Let's get on with the tour, please." Nadia walked past them both back through the opening and into the door on the right. She leaned against the wall and waited for Trent and Mindy to catch up.

"My, my, aren't we fast today." Mindy teased. "This is the laundry room. The door on the back wall leads out to the breezeway and garage."

"What's behind this door?" Nadia pointed to her right.

"That's another bedroom. It has its own bath too." Mindy turned and walked down a small hallway past the laundry room. Nadia and Trent stood in the doorway.

"What is this?"

"This, my dear Nadia, is your walk-in closet."

"This is a walk-in closet? It's so big."

Mindy slid between them, making her way farther down the hall. "Back here is your very own oasis, aka, the master bedroom."

"I hope it has its own bathroom."

"Of course it does!"

"This whole house is huge. Are you sure we can afford this place?"

"You'll be surprised," Mindy smiled. "I'll give you-all some time to talk things over. I'll be outside when you're ready."

"So, what do you think, Nadia? Do you like this place?"

"I do! Did you see that backyard? Everything looks so nice. Do you think we can afford it?"

"Mindy seems to think so." Trent wrapped his arms around her waist and stared into her eyes. "If the price is right, do you want it?"

"Yes, I do."

"Then, let's go get that price."

Nadia and Trent walked out the front door. Mindy was waiting with a grin. "You like it, right?"

"That depends on the price. How much is it?"

"They're asking three-hundred thousand. They will pay all closing costs and a one year home warranty."

"Really?"

"Yes, really. It's a good price. Oh, and you get five acres of land too."

Tingling ran from Nadia's head to her feet. *We can afford this house!* "Why aren't they asking more? They could certainly get it."

Trent cleared his throat and grinned. "Are you questioning God's provision?"

Nadia's eyes met his. "No, I'm not. It's just that you don't hear of this kind of house selling for that kind of money."

"Calm down. I am just playing with you."

"I know." She looked back at Mindy. "We'll need to pray about it. Can we call you tonight, or tomorrow morning?"

"Yes, just don't wait too long."

"We won't."

Nadia plopped down on the couch beside Trent. She leaned her head on his shoulder. "Are you nervous too, or is it just me?"

He tucked her hair behind her ear and gently kissed the top of her head. "I guess I would be lying if I said no, but I don't think I'm as nervous as you."

Nadia grabbed her phone on the first ring. "Hello?"

"Are you sitting down, cause if not you need to be! You're now the proud owners of 7272 Bullock Lane!"

A scream filled the air. "Oh, Mindy! Really?"

"Yes, really. They accepted everything; no counter offer. Strangest thing."

"Not a strange thing, Mindy, a *God* thing!"

She flipped her phone shut and stared at Trent, wide-eyed.

"We got it?"

"Yes, we got it! Oh, Trent, I am so excited."

"I can't believe this is really happening. It all seems so strange."

"It's not a strange thing; it's a God thing, remember?"

Laughter filled the room.

"That it is, Trent. That it is."

They sat beside each other as the last minutes of evening passed.

Chapter 25

Nadia busied herself with work, shopping for miscellaneous items for the house, and wedding planning to help speed up what seemed like the never-ending week. Finally, Friday rolled around, and though she was eating lunch with Trent, her mind was somewhere else.

She blinked her eyes as a hand waved in front of her face.

"Nadia, are you going to answer your phone?"

A faint ringing sound finally reached her ears. She pulled the phone form her pocket. "Hello?"

"Hello, Ms. Lucas; this is Detective Warren. I'm sorry to call you at work, but I figured you were on your lunch break. Is there anyway you can stop by the station before seven tonight? I have some information I need to pass along to you."

"That shouldn't be a problem, Detective."

"Okay, I'll see you this evening."

Trent's eyebrow rose. "What was that about?"

"Detective Warren wants me to come by the station tonight."

"Hopefully he has some good news."

"Hopefully."

The rest of the day passed with little excitement although Nadia kept trying to keep herself focused on the work in front of her.

"Are you ready, Nadia?"

Her head rose. "Ready for what?"

Trent raised his eyebrows. "How am I supposed to be professional when you look at me like that?" He shook his head. "It's five-thirty." He pointed at the clock.

"I didn't realize that. Let me get this folder put up and grab my purse. You can go ahead and go. I'll meet you outside."

Nadia closed the file and placed it in the drawer. She flipped her hair back and placed her purse strap on her shoulder. Looking up, she froze.

"Well, well; who do we have here?"

Nick's empty stare and chilling voice made her skin prickle. Her scream got caught in her throat.

"I see I've left you speechless again." His wicked laugh sent a tremor through her.

"I know it's been a couple weeks, but did you honestly think I'd just give up and disappear? My dear Nadia, that's just not me. Eric found that out the hard way, and I guess so will you."

Her eyes focused on the gun. "I had hoped we could make this work without any trouble. It's sad, really. I think we would've made a good team."

"It never would've worked out, Nick." She forced her courage to buy some time.

"Now, you don't know that. Had you not met-- what's his name-- *Trent*, right? I think everything would have been just fine."

Nadia prayed as he stepped closer. Her eyes darted back and forth between him and the door.

"That's the downside of working late hours, Nadia. You're left here all alone. And I wouldn't advise you to make a run for it; you'd never make it."

Nadia caught a movement past Nick's shoulder. "No, I probably wouldn't. But I don't think you will, either."

Nadia dove behind her desk and peeked around a leg as Nick turned and fired at one of the police officers pouring into the room behind him. Another shot rang out, followed by a thud right beside her. Nick's blond hair covered his face as his body lay in front of her, lifeless. Her heavy, shallow breaths turned into jerking sobs.

"Ms. Lucas, I'm Officer Lee; you can come out now." She grabbed his outstretched hand.

"Nadia!"

She fell into Trent's open arms, burying her face in his chest. He ran his fingers through her hair. "I can't believe he got in here. Thank the Lord the police were still watching the building. But now it's all over, Nadia. It's all over."

The beating heart against her ear drowned out the sounds of the paramedics and officers behind her.

Trent's fingers lifted her chin. "Detective Warren is in the hall. He's motioning for us to come out. Close your eyes; I'll guide you through."

Her emotions warred against her common sense. No way did she want to stay in that room any longer, but her feet protested at the thought of being uprooted from that spot.

Trent wrapped his arm around her waist and she closed her eyes, letting him guide her out.

After talking with Detective Warren and giving their statements, they were told they could go. "I'll call you tomorrow," Detective Warren said.

Nadia looked up into Trent's eyes. "I don't think I'll be much company right now, but will you stay with me?"

"Of course, I will," Trent replied.

Nadia remained quiet on the way home. Her breaths came fast, but shallow, her thoughts occupied by what she witnessed. Her hand trembled as she wiped the tears from her face.

"We're here."

She pressed close to him as they walked, her thoughts replaying the last five months of her life. She willed it to stop, but it wouldn't. She submitted as Trent took off her shoes, pulled back the covers, and lowered her down. She rolled over and faced the wall as he covered her up. His fingers ran through her hair until she finally brought her restless mind to a stop. She welcomed the quiet and was soon asleep.

Chapter 26

The weeks and months passed in a blur. Thanksgiving, Christmas, New Year's and Easter all came and went. It seemed life had just returned to normal when Nadia found herself staring at her reflection in a full-length mirror. The day she had waited for was finally here. The day that kept her faith and hope alive. The man who had stood by her side through it all, not once complaining, now stood out there waiting for her.

Small, delicate curls hung down around her face. Her make-up looked perfect. The off-white, lace-covered gown fell down over the matching heels. A tear rolled down her cheek. *I wish you were here, Mom and Dad. I miss you both so much.*

She jumped at the creak of the door opening.

"You look beautiful, Nadia."

"Thanks, Mindy."

"You ready?"

"Yes."

Nadia walked through the double doors into the sanctuary. All eyes now rested on her as everyone stood up. She didn't notice once her eyes locked with Trent's. The music started to play. Finally, she stood at his side. Everyone sat down as the pastor started the ceremony.

"Welcome family and friends; we are gathered together today to celebrate the union of Trent Ryan Macalister and Nadia Kristine Lucas. Trent, Nadia needs to know without any doubt that you love her, that you'll protect her no matter the cost. She needs your time and communication. Nadia, Trent needs to know you honor and respect him. That you'll have his back and support him. He too needs your love. But the most important thing you both need is a marriage built on the love and foundation of Christ."

He held the rings in the air. "These rings symbolize the circle of love between you both; as you wear them reflect on the wonderful union you both are now creating."

He handed a ring to Trent. "Trent, as you place this ring on Nadia's hand, I now ask you: Do you take this woman to be your lawful wedded wife? Do you promise God, Nadia, and all us here that your arms will be her shelter? Do you promise to support, love, honor, and respect her all the days of your life? If so, please answer, 'I do.'"

"I do."

He handed the ring to Nadia. "Nadia, as you place this ring on Trent's hand, I now ask you: Do you take this man to be your lawful wedded husband? Do you promise God, Trent, and all us here that your arms will be his shelter? Do you promise to support, love, honor, and respect him all the days of your life? If so, please answer, 'I do.'"

"I do."

"Let's bow our heads and pray. Father, we ask that you bless this union with your love, guidance and protection. May the lines of communication always be open, and honesty be ever-present in this relationship. May they forever build their lives together on your solid foundation. In Jesus name, Amen.

By the power vested in me, I now pronounce you Mr. and Mrs. Trent Macalister."

Trent: Everyone has a Past

"Trent Macalister, what have you gotten yourself into this time?" It seems like I couldn't go a day without hearing that. I don't why, but trouble always seemed to attract me. I was raised in a good home with loving parents. But as I hit those awkward, hormonal teenage years—well—something changed. Maybe being an only child had something to do with it. I don't know. The one thing I do know is I'm glad the Lord saved me and set me free.

Enjoy an excerpt from
Trent: Everyone has a Past

Trent: Everyone has a Past

Chapter 1

Trent sat at the bar, with a well-endowed redhead at his side. "Pour me another." He lifted the empty mug into the air.

"Last one, man."

He was sure the bartender was giving him the usual look he'd been told about so many times before. It apparently accompanied the particular tone in the guy's voice. He couldn't tell, though. By the time the tone came, he could never focus enough to find out the truth for himself.

"Yeah, yeah, just pour the drink, will ya?"

"Trent, come on, man," Lee said. "You don't need another drink. It's late and you've had enough."

"Now boys," The redhead flung her hand in the air as if she was swatting at a fly. "Leave the man alone. Let him have his fun."

"Yeah, what the lady said."

Lee shook his head. "I think it's time for the lady to leave as well."

"Go ahead and leave, Lee. I'm fine. I promise." Trent brought the mug towards his mouth, but it missed its intended target. A cool substance dampened his shirt. He jumped. "Oh man!" An abundance of indecent words flowed from between his lips.

"Come on, buddy. Let's go." Lee tossed some cash on the bar and grabbed Trent by the arm before the hot little redhead could convince him to sit back down.

Trent didn't fight it. Like an obedient puppy, he followed his longtime friend outside and across the street to the car. He opened the door, ready to get in.

"Hey, Trent." A gravelly voice resonated from behind him.

He knew that voice. He staggered as he turned and faced in its direction, almost losing his footing. "Yeah, whaddaya want?"

"You're coming with us. Lydia's orders."

"I don't take orders from her. I'm not going anywhere with you. I'm going home and going to bed. Tell *Lydia* I'll call her tomorrow."

The man reached out and grabbed Trent's shirt, yanking him backwards. "Get out of here, Lee," he growled. "He's coming with us."

The last thing Trent remembered was the rough concrete as it scrapped against his skin, leaving behind a faint burning sensation.

He wasn't sure how much time had passed since he had been ruthlessly dragged away from Lee. Truth be told, he didn't care. His life had become a drunken waste of time. He wondered why he was alive. Why he was even born.

A deep breath filled his lungs, followed by an intense jab of pain. He let all his senses, except sight, fully awaken before he opened his eyes. He listened, but didn't hear any sounds. A slight smell drifted his way, but he couldn't calm the pounding in his head long enough to put a name to it. He blinked several times before his eyes adjusted to the bright light that was shining down from the floor lamp next to him. *Okay, wow, why's that there?*

He felt increasing moisture on his forehead. He ran his fingers across his brow to wipe it away and came in contact with a sticky, warm liquid.

What is…?

A wet crimson covered his once-white fingertips. A drop landed on his jeans and soaked through, dampening his leg. "Well isn't this just great."

He scanned the room for something to wipe off with. Not seeing anything, he pulled up the bottom of his shirt and bent down just far enough to reach his head, and then wiped the blood away.

Metal folding chairs, the kind one would see at a church or school function, lined the three walls around him. He knew he wasn't at either of those places. Not in the shape he was in, anyway. One thing he was sure of, he had to get out of the confined room. He didn't mix well with small places. The feeling of being trapped like a caged animal had already kicked in. He wiped the increasing sweat from his palms and forced thoughts of something else through his mind.

"Hello?" His strained voice echoed against the concrete.

If only I could remember how I got here. That's a good reason to stop drinking, I guess. At least I could remember things. He placed his hands on the wall and moved each one up, a little at a time, until he stood on two wobbly legs. He hoped not to aggravate the persistent pounding in his head, but he had failed. The heavy beating of metal drums rang out even more.

He glanced towards the door. Freedom was on the other side of it. It had to be. He took several steps before stopping at the round table that stood just shy of the exit. A pale blue envelope lay at the edge. The scent, stronger now, entered his nostrils.

Jasmine.

Trent willed his legs to keep moving, but curiosity won against his common sense. He picked up the envelope, held it to his nose, and inhaled. The familiar scent tugged at his heart, yet at the same time brought on feelings of utter disgust.

An unpleasant squeak pierced the stillness. He sought it out, finding the answer in a short, stocky man who now stood holding the door open, blocking the exit. *Wonderful.* Trent's lip curled up in frustration as his eyes narrowed. He glared at the stranger in front of him, taking note of the smirk plastered on his face. *There goes my chance of getting out of here.*

"Mr. Macalister. Glad to see you're up and moving. Ms. Winston was getting a little concerned. I see you found her note. Did you read it yet?"

"Does it look like I've read it yet? It's not open, is it?" He flipped it over so that the back was facing the man.

"So no, I haven't," he answered in a firm voice. *And why would I want to? The woman is wicked.*

"Well, that's fine. You'll have time to, later on. Bring it with you and follow me."

"Follow you? Where?"

"You are so full of questions, Mr. Macalister."

Everything about this man caused irritation to course through Trent's bruised body. He'd wanted nothing more than to beat his over-confident attitude right out of him. He thought twice about it before coming to the conclusion that it would only cause more trouble for him. He had enough of that already. Instead, he found a bit of satisfaction in the scene as it played out in his mind.

The man cleared his throat. Trent refocused his attention, disappointed at the interruption of his thoughts.

"I can't answer them, but if you follow me, I will take you to the one who can."

The last thing he wanted to do was follow this man. He knew who was waiting for him. He didn't want to see her. Not now. Not ever.

Trent took one step at a time, careful not to let his legs betray him. Picking himself up off the floor hadn't been at the top of his list of things to do today. He gestured towards the door, his voice full of arrogance. "Lead on."

They walked in silence down the hallway until they arrived at an elevator. *Of course, there'd only be one way out, why would I think any differently.* The stocky man pushed the button and turned on his heels, his stubby finger pointed up towards Trent.

"I think you'll need a chair if you're expecting that to reach my face." A gruff laugh followed Trent's remark.

"We'll see who's laughing in the end, boy." He nodded his head towards the elevator as the door opened. "Take it up to the second floor. Ms. Winston is waiting for you." The man pulled out his phone and stepped back as the door slid shut.

Trent didn't get the chance to hear what was said.

He wasn't sure he wanted to. The thought of being in *Ms. Winston's* presence again was bad enough. His parents' warned him about women like her. Women who like to devour young men like some sort of prey. They lay waiting to ambush, striking at just the right moment, which apparently for her, was now, thanks to his bad decisions. Regret washed over him. *Why didn't I listen?*

His hand gripped the silver railing as the elevator door opened at the second floor. The warm air, filled with the scent of jasmine, flooded in around him. A man resembling a brick wall stood on the other side of the opening, dressed in a black suit. *This should be fun.* Trent released his grip, one finger at a time, allowing his white knuckles to return to their normal color, and stepped out.

The man placed his hand on Trent's shoulder and pushed him forward. "Move!"

A searing pain filled Trent's head. Every noise was magnified. He wanted to cover his ears, but his pride wouldn't let him. He regained his composure and walked towards the closed door that was off to the right. He clenched his jaw at the man's knocks against the solid wood.

A smooth, sultry voice slithered through the cracks. "Come in."

He shuddered at the memory of how enticing that voice once was. How intriguing, pleasing. Not anymore. The days of longing to hear it were gone. He hated it. His fingertips pressed tightly against his palm as warmth flooded his face.

"Mr. Macalister, it's so nice to see you again. I wasn't sure I would. You look … rough." She pointed to the seat across from her desk. "Please sit down. We have so much to talk about." She nodded towards the man in the doorway, signaling for his dismissal.

The latch clicked and intensified the closing in of the small room. *What is it with people and tiny places?* His breathing increased. *Calm down, get control of yourself. If she sees you sweat, she'll have you for dinner.*

"You're being so formal today, *Ms. Winston,* what's the occasion?" Trent lowered his body into the chair. He stared at the women across from him. Her strawberry blonde hair was pulled back on each side, revealing her perfectly round face. Her bangs lay across her forehead in a straight line just above her ice-blue eyes.

A sneer set upon her rose-colored lips. He hated those lips. So inviting. So dangerous. A person could only guess how many times they uttered one lie after another. Sadly, he knew his lips weren't any different. He wasn't sure which bothered him more, her deception, or his own.

For the first time, as he sat there in the silence, he realized just how different their worlds were. There she sat, in her designer clothes, looking every bit the part of a glamorous model. Her make-up was perfect, and not hair out of place. While he, on the other hand, sported a blood stained T-shirt and worn-out blue jeans. Not to mention, his hair. He could only imagine what it looked like, matted blood and all. *I don't care. All right, maybe I do, but I'm not going to let her know that. I refuse to be intimidated by this stunning, yet deceitful, woman any longer.*

Her rhythmic finger-drumming on the desk drew

his eyes to hers. "What do you want, Lydia? Or wait, should I call you, *Ms. Winston* today?"

"I see you haven't lost your disrespectful attitude."

"I only have a disrespectful attitude towards those who've done me wrong. Which you certainly fit that category, don't you think?"

Lydia stood, revealing every curve under her tight black dress. She walked around her desk, stopped in front of him, and leaned back, arms crossed. "I wouldn't say that. It's not my fault you were so eager to prove what a bad boy you were. I'm sorry, maybe I should say *are*, what a bad boy you *are*. You believed every little thing I told you. It's actually a little sad—you were so easy."

The warmth in his cheeks intensified at her mocking, but truthful, words. *Oh, how I wish I could deny that.* His grip tightened around the arm of the chair, smashing the small cushion under the red material.

"I guess you're right, Lydia. It is my fault. But I will *not* be a part of your entertainment anymore. I won't be at your beck and call to do whatever you want. When you want. I'm finished."

"Is that what you think, it'll be that easy to walk away from me?"

"No, it's not what I think. It's what I know. I'm done with this cat and mouse game, Lydia. I want out."

"It's not wise for one to be so hasty in making decisions. We've known each other for several years. Why don't we talk about things and see if we can't come to an agreement?"

"I don't want to talk about things. I told you, I'm finished. There is no agreement to come to."

"Ah, I see. Where do you think the money for your booze will come from, if you walk away from us now?"

Trent stood up, causing the chair to tip over behind him. "Walk away from us? There's no *us*, Lydia. There's only you." His voice grew loud. "It's always been you. It shouldn't be hard to find some other poor sap to take my place. Not that you really need one. "

Lydia's pale cheeks turned cherry-red as her warm breath collided against his face. He got to her. They both knew it. Her finger was mere centimeters from his chest. "You may think that you can walk away from me easily, but you, unfortunately, are mistaken, *Trent.* You owe me, remember?"

He did. But this life was one he couldn't stand living anymore. He was losing control of himself. He didn't like that. Not knowing what happened the night before was the last straw. It had to stop. The old Trent, the guy who was reliable, caring, and sure of himself, was on a pretty steady pace at disappearing.

"I remember, Lydia. I will get you the money, and then I expect all communications between us to stop. I don't want to hear from you anymore."

"Really? Well then, how do you plan on getting my money? You can't afford your drinking habit without me." She walked back around her desk, sat down, and propped up her feet.

"I don't know yet, but I'll get it all right. Just leave it at that." A shiver ran down his spine at the smug look on her face.

"Tell you what. I'll give you three days to pay me back the full five thousand."

He fought the urge to squirm under her gaze. Sure, she was a powerful woman, he knew that, but he refused to let her win.

"If you don't, I'll find you, and rest assured, our next meeting will be less pleasant than the one you had with my boys a couple years ago. I trust you remember that one well, don't you?"

Trent tried to fight off the memory of that night, but it was no use. Every part of it filled his mind —the air, the smells, the sound. The pain. He shuddered as he was transported back in time.

Trent had walked up the sidewalk to his apartment building after he had returned home from a weekend party at Lydia's. Someone had grabbed a hold of him. He spun around and had come face to masked-face with his attacker. The cold air stung his cheeks as a searing pain traveled across his mid-section.

He woke in a hospital bed, his uncle asleep in the chair beside him. The beeping from the machine next to him stirred his uncle from sleep. He quickly sat up and looked over at his nephew.

Trent started to speak, but was cut off by a nurse entering the room.

"All right, Mr. Macalister, what are you up to in here?" She walked over to the monitor, wrote something down, and then checked him over.

"Is he okay?"

"Yes, Mr. White. His numbers came back down pretty quickly. He could have been having a bad dream or memory. Those are pretty normal things that can happen after something like he's been through. If you need anything, don't hesitate in pressing the call button," she said before she walked out.

"Do you want to talk, Trent?"

He gave no response, lying there as though he was lifeless.

Moments later, he heard the ring of his phone. "Uncle Clark, will you please hand me my phone?"

Clark sat motionless for a second before he reached into his pocket, took out the phone, and placed it in Trent's upturned palm.

The screen displayed the number of the last person he wanted to speak to. He had no doubt this had something to do with their big disagreement that had turned into the main entertainment at her party.

"Well, well, Lydia. To what do I owe this very late call to?" he asked, weakness in his voice.

"Now Trent, why do you always have to have such an attitude? We're friends, remember?"

"What do you want, Lydia?"

"Straight to the point. That's what you want?"

"Yes, that's what I want."

"Fine, then. I was just making sure my boys left you the message I sent. Wouldn't want any misinformation, or crossed wires, you know."

"No, we wouldn't want that. Your boys did leave a message, come to think about it. But I'm not sure it's the one you were counting on."

"Oh, and why's that?"

"I answered the phone, didn't I?"

Seconds passed before her response reached his ear. "You have a point. Next time—rest assured—my message will be carried out to completion."

He shifted in the chair and pushed the memories aside as he returned his focus back to conniving woman in front of him.

"Yes, I remember it clearly."

The corner of her mouth rose ever so slightly. "Perfect. I'll see you soon."

"If only that weren't true." He reached for the knob, but the door swung open before he made contact with it. The guard stood, waiting for him to walk through.

His muscles constricted at the feel of a soft hand on his shoulder. *How can something so soft, be so callous?*

"I'm sure you didn't mean that."

Oh, yes I did.

"On the off chance you might want to find your way out of here, I suggest you follow Mr. Willow. Oh, and Trent, don't forget." She held up one finger at a time, stopping at the third. "Three days."

Stay informed at www.KellyHagen.weebly.com

Acknowledgments

A sincere thank you to the following:

My Lord and Savior, Jesus Christ – Without you this book wouldn't have been written. May it touch the lives of those who read it.

My family – Thank you for all your support and encouragement.

My friends and fellow authors – Thank you for your input. It helped me greatly.

TreasureLine Publishing – Thank you for working with me and bringing everything together.

My readers – Remember God always directs our paths. May your faith and trust in Him grow more each day.

About the Author

Kelly Hagen is a wife, and mother of three. She's also the author of *Jake and Jesus*, a children's book that teaches children that they too can have a friendship with Jesus. Kelly enjoys spending time with her family and friends, reading her Bible, and listening to music

Kelly would love to hear from you at her website, www.kellyhagen.weebly.com and on Facebook at www.facebook.com/AuthorKellyHagen